THE SHORT, SHORT-STORY

Omnibus-1

Edited by
BERNARD BLOCK

iUniverse, Inc.
Bloomington

The Short, Short-Story
Omnibus-1

Our first publication, "The Sleeping Girl on the Couch" is a 218-page E-book suspense-thriller that takes place In the field of art, with mysterious and terrorist implications. Special price of $5.88. To obtain a copy, buy it from E-Books or contact us at karandell@juno.com.

iUniverse books may be ordered through booksellers or by contacting:

iUniverse
1663 Liberty Drive
Bloomington, IN 47403
www.iuniverse.com
1-800-Authors (1-800-288-4677)

ISBN: 978-1-4759-7092-0 (sc)
ISBN: 978-1-4759-7093-7 (e)

Printed in the United States of America
iUniverse rev. date: 1/11/2013

DISCLAIMER

Many of these 500-2,000 word fiction short stories contain a lot of true information and statements that have been picked up from researching various media by the authors. All the stories have "twist" endings, similar to the famous short-story writer O.Henry who wrote in the beginning of the 20th century.

The stories included are figments of the authors' imagination and written for your enjoyment in the short, short-story form. If you have written a short, short-story and would like it to be included in the Omnibus-2 edition, E-mail it to us at KARANDELL@JUNO.COM for consideration. There is no reading fee, and if accepted you will be paid from the Omnibus-2 royalties earned by Karandell Corp (the publishers).

BERNARD BLOCK, *Editor*

Dedicated to my three daughters,
Andrea, Ellen and Karen

TABLE OF CONTENTS

How To Steal A Condo

by Milton Beer

Bud and John Brown were at their friend's sumptuous swimming pool enjoying themselves.

Bud says, "John, did you hear about my condo assessment coming up?"

"No," John replies, "What's up?"

"So you haven't heard? I might be assessed for thousands of dollars for various repairs, and the possibility that we will be going into the real estate business by building some new condos where we have empty land. There is even talk about a golf course being built!"

"What? Why would you want to pay thousands to the condo, especially the part about a golf course? You don't play the game."

"Well, that's what I heard, and I don't like it either. I think I should find out a bit more because my information could be a rumor only.

"Brown and Brown, Condo Legal Lawyers and Real Estate Developers. How can I help you," said the cute blonde at the front reception desk as she picked up the phone? She had heavy eye make-up and big breasts stuffed into a sexy dress that showed her best attributes for all to see. Ted Worth heard her because he was sitting very close to the desk waiting for the company's vice president, Bud Brown.

"Yes, the Browns are here," said the receptionist, "But which one would you like to speak to?" She paused, waiting for a reply. "Yes, John Brown is the President, but I'm afraid he's been on the phone the better part of the last hour and I can't promise you when he will be free. I'll contact him when he's finished and find out when he will be able to set up an appointment. May I please have your name, and your company so I can give him this information?" she said while taking off a piece of paper from a pad next to the phone.

"Yes…Mr. Oscula…oh, of the Cortenga Tribe of Indians. I got it. And your title, sir, at the company?... Oh, Chief, I gotcha. Where can you be reached Sir Chief?"…"Got it, 456-789-0000. That's an easy number to remember."

After hanging up, she put the note in one of the mail slot boxes behind her. She turned towards me since she observed I was listening intently to the conversation, and said, "That's an interesting person I would like to meet." While fluttering her eyes at me, "But my life is basically dull!"

That, of course, was ludicrous. She was a sensuous blonde with only her body the one asset that will probably help her latch on to someone with a lot of money to keep a dream lifestyle she would like, and not have to use her brains much.

A buzzer sounded on her desk and she picked up the phone. "Yes, I'll send him now." She turned to me and said, "Mr. Bud Brown is ready for you. It's the door on the left."

"My name is Ted Worth, Mr. Brown. Remember I spoke to you last week about needing a developer for a piece of land I own in Costa Rico. You said you do work in other countries, I believe? Since you are nodding your head, let me tell you what I want to do."

With that I described the type of development I wanted—Mediterranean-style apartments surrounding a middle patio. I felt there was a need for this type of development since many Americans were now moving to this country and wanted what they were used to at home.

"Yes, Mr. Worth," Bud Brown replied, "I believe we can help you."

As Chief Oscula walked into John Brown's suite for his appointment, he was followed by two other men whom he introduced as his executives. After sitting down, Mr. Brown said, "Glad to meet you Chief, I am well aware of your tribe since I've been living near the Cortenga casino for many years. What can I do for you?"

The Chief stood, and started to speak.

"A few years ago our tribe's casino/hotel wanted to expand but we had a hard time getting good help because while we paid them well, their living costs in this area were very high. We then solved the housing problem by offering new employees nearby residences we owned privately, and allowed them to pay much smaller rent than anywhere else in the area.

"For the last ten years that approach worked, but eventually we ran out of nearby homes and could not find any closer. A quarter mile away we had purchased a few homes in a 500-unit condo association, but we couldn't find too many more.

"At the same time we wanted to construct a golf course which would entice more out-of-town guests interested in the sport to our hotel/casino and offer lower golf fees than the already existing surrounding ones. However, that too produced a problem since empty land in the area was scarce, and the price for these lands were quite high.

"We looked at the possibility of buying more condos at this 500-unit condo which still had a great deal of empty land available; however, there were some problems. For instance, an owner could not rent out more than five residences at any one time. That problem was easily solved by forming 20 different corporations, with different Indian owners which allowed us to own 100 residences in this 500-unit condo, which we used extensively to offer to our new employees.

"We decided the only way we could get a majority of votes to gain control of the Association was to buy 251 units…and then we would appoint enough members to control the Association's Board. The only way to get people to sell was not only to offer more than the average price for their units, but to start a rumor that someone was buying and renting more units than usual, and that the condo was considering going into the real estate business and use the available vacant land to build new homes, thus increasing the congestion in an already busy place. That could be quite costly.

"In addition, the most intriguing part of this scheme... oops...plan...would be to start a rumor that a golf course was going to be built on the rest of our vacant land, and that assessments were going to go sky high to support all of this new start-up activity, *which is exactly what we started to do.*

"Slowly, the offering price for these once high-priced residences dropped and we were able to buy enough by last year to control the Board of Directors...thus we could do what we wanted...like raising assessments to $100,000 to pay for our developing costs. It worked once we got control.

"Properties started coming to us quite rapidly, and the prices were dropping more than we thought would happen."

The Chief stopped talking, took a drink of water from a glass filled which was perched on John Brown's desk, and continued.

"We are here, today, Mr. Brown, since your company represents many condominiums and have had a hand in development work. We wanted to learn if there are any new laws which would prevent us from doing what we have done already and what we planned in the future, and if our Board of Directors we control has exceeded its authority? From our investigations we believe we have not violated any laws."

"Off the top of my head," John Brown responded, "I don't believe that your plan violates any laws presently. In fact it is a most ingenious one that you thought of a few years ago, and have planned it well. I'll do some checking, but I am sure it's okay.

The following year, the Brown brothers were at a wedding celebration with their wives and were having a great time as they usually did. They started talking about business when their wives were away. John said to Bud, "What's up?"

"Remember that story I told you last year about the rumors I heard? Well, I've just been assessed by my condo for $100,000 to cover some new units for our vacant land and the construction of an 18-hole golf course on the rest of the property. So I guess those rumors were true. I'll probably sell since there is a company offering rather nice prices for our condo units...although for far less than they were selling for two years ago."

"Oh, Bud," John exclaimed. "They were my clients and I couldn't tell you anything about what they were doing because of the *client-lawyer relationship* which forbids me to disclose such information. Sorry, but I'm sure you'll find another place to live...but don't forget to investigate thoroughly before you buy!"

Jordan & Johnathan

By Robert Bonon

My name is Bill.

My grandson, Johnathan, just got married in a small wedding with many friends present, and very little of my family members attending.

Johnathan and his "wife," Jordan, met at the University of Virginia when they were both taking the same economics class. They clicked on the very first day of the class. After spending three more years at the University, they moved into a small apartment as roommates when they started working in their chosen professions.

They had a wonderful life before their marriage, and after this wedding, as well. One thing I remember from the "wedding" was when one of the grandparents got up to say a few remarks, ending them by reading a passage from the 1984 Reader's Digest…"Remember, when you get married you are really marrying three people—the person they were, the person they are now, and the person they become after getting married."

It was so true. They had a terrific marriage, and they became a wonderful couple. However, one thing was missing. They couldn't have children. This eventually was solved when Johnathan and his "wife" adopted a pair of twins who are now three years old; it was the best thing that could possibly happen in their young married life.

It was not easy to obtain adopted children. They finally had all the necessary paperwork okayed from various state agencies, but it took up to eleven hysterical months to complete the process.

Johnathan and Jordan immediately started saving up enough money to send the twins to the college of their choice…and remember, this was two at the same time. You are talking about a couple of hundred thousand dollars for the so-called "good" college over four years. And, you could never tell the costs could be more if any one of the twins decided to extend their education (and it could be two), who went on to post graduate work!

They also became involved with my personal advisor on how to pass on their wealth to these children, as well as to each other.

Once we had a long talk one evening; they told me later during this conversation on how they thought about their life in general, especially since one was Jewish and one was Catholic. They worked this religious problem out when they decided they would let the twins choose what they wanted to do, even accepting the fact that they may pick neither of the religions of their parents. They reached this conclusion when one of them discovered a reference book in the Library called "Guide to the Gods" which detailed the 20,000 Gods from thousands of years ago before this current crop. So there were plenty of Gods around to pick from.

Politically, Johnathan and Jordan felt the same way.

They would not try to influence the twins but would let them think for themselves concerning politicians who promise too much without offering any details to solve problems. They decided that they would not voice their own opinions about gays, lesbians and transvestites or any other sexual differences. They reiterated that the twins would have to make up their own minds and evaluate the ways of the world on any subject.

To this day, Johnathan and Jordan are still in love and have a busy life together, and probably will for the rest of their lives since they are involved in many causes.

When they reach their 50th anniversary they still plan to celebrate this high point as man and "wife" even though you might think they were two men who had married.

Sorry, folks. Johnathan's wife is a wonderful female even though her name happens to be Jordan, a male-like name that could be used for either sex. As a famous saying that has been passed on to many generations states… "Don't judge a book by its cover"…the same goes for names!

There's No Place Like Home

By Babette Pennington

"I think I've solved my problem," said a female heroin homeless person before collapsing in front of an Emergency Room in her local home town hospital.

After many hospital admissions in the past twenty years, this heroin-addicted homeless person says, "My life over the past two decades can be summed up with a devastating story…hostels, drugs, hospitals, streets, drinking, hospitals, streets, drinking, hospitals, and so on, always ending up in the hospital." She does believe now that she has an answer to her problem.

It was found that long-term homeless people are easy to help, and it's an open secret in Emergency Room Departments and in-patient wards that there is often a lack of compassion among staff for homeless people. Most of these medical people believe that with complex physical and mental health problems, brought on by drug or alcohol abuse, they acknowledge that these long-term health problems have been brought on by the patients themselves.

"They're like ping-pong balls," said one healthcare worker. "They usually return to the place where they started and never seem to end the game."

It's true since homeless addicts always go AWOL and don't like explaining themselves or ask for help if pushed; they flip out because doctors and nurses don't know how to deal with them, saying, "So they fix us medically then chuck us back out on the streets"

Homeless people must cost hospitals lots of money for the care they provide, especially when they know that they have no place to go, come back routinely, and stay twice as long as any other patient. To them it's like a home of sort.

Take one notorious case of a Jane Doe who has likely cost a hospital more than eight times that of the housed population. The homeless population is admitted to hospitals more than four times as often, and stay two times as long because they have nowhere to move on to and because they are twice as sick.

Take England, for example. These hard-to-reach groups can be boiled down to two simple facts; there are around 40,500 homeless people in this country, and altogether they generate secondary care costs of about $85 million pounds

A new project has been proposed. A group of social workers, mental health teams, drug and alcohol workers discharge-liaison teams and housing specialists tailoring personal, multi-agency care packages for each homeless patient in a hospital. While in its infant stage, it's too hard to see if this approach works

"I've heard about the program," the collapsed patient summarized four days later when she was more alert to her problem. "But I've tried many programs throughout the past two decades, and none of them seem to work for me.

"I have a new idea that makes it simple. Keeping me in one place for a long time makes it less costly than a hospital, and use that solution because nothing else seems to work.

"How can there be a simple solution to such a difficult problem. Here's how it works. ***Pass the buck somewhere that does not expect a permanent solution to a plan.***

"I've been thinking very hard about my problem, and I've come to the conclusion that nothing works in the present condition. It would be an idea that cost less than hospitals charge, offers a more permanent one that will satisfy the public as to costs and solutions.

"NO, it's not offering me a suicidal solution, although that's not a bad idea, but not one I would agree with at the moment.

"The solution is to eliminate all the healthcare workers, as well as hospitals and other places similar to them, and come up with an idea that would appeal to everyone. Let me commit a crime that throws me into prison for awhile, like maybe five to ten years, and keep doing the some type of crime in the jail to extend my stay more permanently so I won't be kicked out.   Therefore, I will be out of harm's way, won't hurt anyone else, my family will know where I am at all times, and I'll have plenty of company. I'll be kept busy working at some kind of job, I get time off for myself out in a courtyard at least one hour a day which should be good for my health if I exercise properly, and I'll be treated at a healthcare facility for a cost far less than I would be at a regular hospital…and probably get rid of my addiction-prone diseases."

And, of course, I won't be a homeless person anymore!

CREDITWORTHY

by Unknown Name

"You're pre-approved!"

"$50,000 available credit limit."

"Low APR (Annual Percentage Rate)…only 2.9% on balance transfers!"

Whew. Another credit card solicitation! Over the years I've had many.

No wonder. According to a recent story I read in a famous magazine, there were over six billion credit-card solicitations a year. Families now carry a credit balance on the average of $9,312. A consumer who owes $5,000 at a 16% interest minimum usually pays 2% each month towards their bill; this will take 36 years to pay off, and will be rewarding the credit-card companies $9,329 interest over that time. Now I can understand why there are billions of solicitations to tempt us.

I have applied for a few, especially when I could get a card on a NO-FEE basis, and at the same time receive back a percentage, usually 1% cash on total purchases annually. I really like the cards that offer 3.5% back on purchases from supermarkets, gas stations and drug stores. Sometimes I'm offered airline miles, or points to buy products sponsored by major companies, like GM, Delta Airlines, etc. I really like the cash back ones the best...it's like saving money in the bank and forgetting it was there.

Eventually, I converted all my credit cards to just the NO FEE-CASH BACK type.

I can remember living off credit cards when I was unemployed for a while. It kept the wolf away from the door. I built up an "I-owe-you-credit-card-company" large balance that took me years to pay off after I was back at work.

But it sure helped my *credit-worthiness!*

I truthfully can say that without those credit cards I would have been in big trouble, financially. But thank goodness I had a good credit payoff background prior to that period of my life.

Over the past few years, I used my credit card to such an extent that if I took out $100 in cash from the bank it would last me at least three months or more. The cash was used where credit cards were not accepted. Once in awhile I would get a discount at a restaurant who gave one if you gave them cash. Everything else I had to pay was done mostly through my credit cards, or with a not-often-used check.

My credit history is excellent now since I continue to receive credit-card solicitations and applications by the dozens, every week.

Since I needed a way to raise money for my retirement fund, I decided I would use my "old buddy"...Mr. Credit Card...to help.

I learned that the credit-card business was a large

one, close to $900 billion (and rising rapidly) in charges annually through more than three billion plastic cards ranging from people with bad credit to the wealthiest American Express cardholder. Defaults and bankruptcies run into the millions of dollars, if not billions. I'm not sure about the figures since they are a closely-guarded secret in the industry.

It was about to get some dollars higher!

Yes, you guessed right. I decided to really take advantage of all those credit-card solicitations I received in the mail to help build the fund-raising dollars I would need to help my retirement funds have enough to take care of me for years.

Since I was solicited practically every day by some bank or company that pleaded to take out their credit card because of my excellent rating, I decided it was time to make my move, one that concerned building up my fund-raising account.

For a few years after I initiated my action plan, I accepted the generous solicitations to open a credit-card account with the many banks and companies that offered pre-approvals and other benefits…all, of course, with NO FEE charges and with cash credits applied monthly. I studiously paid each credit card fully and on time to build up the confidences of the lenders. They, in turn, offered me more lines of credit and cash advances, saying how much they appreciated my business.

I spent a great deal of time on my computer keeping track of all my transactions. But it was worth it.

By the time you read this story, all of my cash advance checks will have been used, and product purchases made on the many, many credit cards I have accumulated will have reached the highest possible level during the past 45 days (or just before payments are due). I even may be a few days late. Of course, the monies cashed from my advance checks will be forwarded overseas to an unknown account and all the goodies I purchased will have been pawned and the cash turned over to my fund-raising goals. I will have to leave the country, but that has always been part of the plan.

I want to thank the credit-card lenders for their help toward making my fund raising endeavors successful. Couldn't have done it without them!

Oh, yes. In case the credit-card personnel who read this story haven't surmised—I have no plans to pay off their company's last statement. Nor do I plan to charge anything in the future, or accept any credit-card pleas to accept their devilish product. And, all my U.S. checking and bank accounts will have been closed, too.

There goes my ***credit-worthiness***, but at least I won't be receiving any more invitations to open a credit-card account!

ANONYMOUS.

POTTY TRAINING CAN BE COSTLY

by Joyce Brenner

**(From an exclusive interview
with a reporter from the daily newspaper)**

"I'm not a bad mother," said Evelyn Escal,"

"I'm just a molested, abused-by-boyfriends, overburdened mother and recovering marijuana/cocaine addict raising four children in a bug-infested, one-bedroom apartment on child support payments. I just got frustrated, wouldn't you?

"The prosecutor painted me as a cruel and calculating monster. So what if I beat my youngest, and finally super-glued her hands to the wall as sort of a punishment? She deserved it because I became very frustrated with my daughter's potty-training issue and I had to do something besides spanking her often. I figured if I taught her a real lesson, it would straighten things out...and it worked.

"The judge said I wasn't sorry for what I did, but that I was sorry for myself and not the child I tortured. He was wrong. It's true I beat my daughter many times, smacked her around a bit, but nothing worked. The super-glue worked and she did what she had to do.

"They arrested me when the maintenance man came into help and saw what I did. The nosy superintendent should have kept her mouth shut instead of reporting my actions to the police. She wasn't in my shoes. Betcha you would have done something dramatic, too!

"Anyway, my lawyer said if I pleaded guilty, and with my unfortunate background I wouldn't get too much time in jail…and the State would probably put my kids into good foster homes and give them a chance to a better life than I could…and that I may be able to see them in the not-too-distant future."

Speaking with the prosecutor, this reporter learned that he was only seeking a 15-25 year sentence, which meant Evelyn could possibly get out in 10 years for good behavior and for pleading guilty to the charges since she would be saving the County a lot of money for a guilty-plea, uncontested trial. She always could appeal the verdict and sentence and ask for a full-blown trial anytime in the future.

Evelyn thought this over and decided to plead guilty. She was amazed on what happened after at the sentencing.

"Ms. Escal. I believe that you are a monster for treating your 2-year old the way you did which led to her being in a coma. That was cruel and unusual punishment, no matter how you felt or the amount of so-called 'love' you had for your children," the judge said before sentencing.

"I, therefore, am sentencing you to the maximum the law will allow under the circumstances to 99 years in prison!"

What a shock to Ms. Escal. It was a bombshell and set a record for "Justice." Afterwards it was learned the judge was concerned about her beating the 2-year-old child almost to death, and that his decision was based on the brutality of the attacks and available punishment. Sometimes you can guess wrong, can't you?

"I want everyone to know that I am not a monster; I love my kids.," she said before leaving the courtroom.

(AUTHOR'S NOTE: This short story was written from actual events that were reported in the October 18, 2012 edition of Florida's SunSentinel)

CRUISING FOR GOLD

by Ralph Abernath

My wife and I love to cruise.

It's the best buy for the vacation dollars you spend. Great food, marvelous entertainment, great service, a chance to visit various foreign countries…and you even meet some interesting people who like to talk about themselves.

Better yet. It's the best way we have found to get "prospects" when they are unaware of your true intentions…to relieve them of a few of their valuables, **but never on a cruise ship**.

No, my wife and I use a different method. We don't relieve them of their valuables on board, but from their home while they cruise. This provides us with a great alibi, too!

Even our travel agent who is an accomplice is totally unaware of the role he/she plays.   Let me explain… really it's very simple.

The first thing we do is to review the ship's layout and pinpoint where the most expensive cabins are situated from brochures and information supplied by our travel agent, or the cruise company itself.

Prior to boarding, we have obtained different passports for each trip we take…that's four times a year…so that authorities do not tie in the fact that we are at sea when a consistent number of robberies occur to cruise passengers' homes on land. After we board the ship, we pass by the cabins we have selected and note their names on the door (not all ships do this) so we are very selective which cruise lines we sail on.

Over the next few days we make a few calls to the occupants of the cabins selected to determine where they live. What we say exactly to obtain this information is a secret we will not expose. We also make calculated attempts to meet these passengers in various ways—at the pool, during games played on board, trips to tourist sites, in the dining rooms and at entertainment venues, and especially at "art auctions" where they may be buying expensive artwork. We go anywhere we can come in contact with our selected "targets and become extremely friendly which helps obtain more information than they normally would not expose.

We have set up a modus operandi to use on the land portion of our endeavor. We have found a felon who has been convicted of burglary and wants to continue in this chosen profession, but with a bit more information than normally found.

For instance, we can supply this person exactly when the target's home will be empty because they will be on a cruise with us. We may also have developed information concerning the presence of a burglar alarm, dog ownership, visitors, house sitters, police checks…all important things a house burglar needs to know. We might even know how wealthy these cruisers are by looking up the value of homes in their area through media sources, possible income and any other news of value we can pass onto our land operator.

We bring our portable computer with us to keep in touch with our accomplice on land, providing there are wireless capabilities aboard. Most ships today have Internet connections so it's easy to maintain contact with whomever you wish anywhere in the world. We can also be in contact with our land person by phone when we arrive at ports the ship stops at while cruising.

Advising our accomplice as soon as possible, usually within 3-5 days into a cruise, preferably the long ones since we might need extra days for our land accomplice to travel long distances to reach our "targeted" cruiser's home, and also give him time to get the lay of the land before entry.

We also use tactics to learn what especially important things are in the home; you would be surprised what people tell you on board cruise ships and how they like to boast about themselves and their accomplishments... and valuable collections they have gathered due to their wealth.

It's absolutely amazing what people will talk about when you become "friends" on a cruise.

Financing our cruising, other living costs, and doing some fund-raising activity for outside groups is important to us. So far we have been quite successful; although since we have increased our activity and are now going cruising six times a year, our land contact is becoming more demanding and asking for more of a cut on the dollars we get for selling what he has stolen through the "exclusive" broker we have supplied.

We'll get to solve that problem when the time is necessary to do so.

Meanwhile, we are sorry that we can't include our picture in this story. We really don't want to let you know when we may be targeting **you** on your next cruise!

NOTE: This story was written a few years ago. Would you believe that what was told in the story actually happened a few years after it was written

It's a Dog's Life

by Joan Camir

"Let me tell you about this new program we started at the hospital where I am executive administrator."

"There are a group of dogs working a good deal with hospital patients. They even have their own Facebook page on the Internet.

"They deal with patients in hospital rehab programs who are recuperating from strokes, heart attacks, car accidents, cancer, to name a few of the illnesses with which these dogs are involved.

"It's kind of a holistic-approved healing program.

"In one instance, our hospital had six golden retrievers who were obtained from an Assistance Dog Program which cost the hospital $5,000 each for their training the first 18 months of their lives.

"Getting a full-scale hospital-based dog therapy program off the ground was the biggest challenge. It had been recommended as a unique therapy tool by a hospital system task force on healing experiences in a concept unheard of...and had plenty of critics. It was a hard sell for the hospital administrators because most people when they think of dogs, think germs.

"Program advocates developed protocols and procedures, including frequent hand washing and grooming that passed the hospital's infectious disease specialists. One hospital administrator advised that the dogs had been used three years since they joined the staff and there have been no reports of them spreading germs or behaving improperly; it was reported that infections went down after their introduction.

"It was found that the therapeutic value of dogs has been way more than expected. Some people are very distressed after an illness or injury, so the dog is a nice way to give a daunting task a little twist,

"There were six dogs on our staff and each one had a special talent. One dog named "Nutmeg" serves kids and play a rambunctious game of fetch. Another, called "Liz", works with rehab patients and retrieves shoes from the closet and practices balance with rope tugs. There's one dog named "Pumpkin" who works with cardiac rehab patients. She accompanies patients on treadmill walks. Another, named "Lucy," is used in obstetrics, surgical, orthopedic rehab patients and likes to participate in group behavior therapy. "Allen," not only works with postsurgical care patients in the hospital, but at an associated nursing home for rehab residents. The last dog of this six-team group, "Compass," specializes in sports medicine, as well as speech therapy and pediatric rehab patients.

"Each breed has a different personality. Some are a kid at heart, some energetic and playful, others are calm and patient and sweetly coach patients through therapy.

"There are about six handlers per dog and between

potty breaks and naps the animals get plenty of attention. They have their own Facebook page and each has a *Bark Line* answering machine so patients and doctors can call in and request a visit ahead of time.

"The dogs' schedules are usually booked solid. By the end of the day when it's time to go home, these celebrity pets are just another member of the family one of the handlers noted.

One incident stood out in the Administrator's mind. It was like a tit-for-tat incident.

"One of the three-year-old dogs, 'Nutmeg', got hit by a car and was brought to a next door vet hospital. This dog had been working with seven-year-old 'Niami" who had been receiving chemotherapy for cancer…and the dog made the treatment bearable.

"When Niami found out that Nutmeg was in dog rehab, she insisted, no demanded, to be taken to him. When she got there everything was in reverse…Niami petted the dog, kissed him, stroked him for hours. Every day we had to take her to the hospital, and she gave the dog just the same treatment she had received from him. ***He got better faster than ever!***

THE BRIDGE OF OPPORTUNITY ONLY KNOCKS ONCE

by Jerome Jackson

"I love the game of bridge," Jerimiah said while attending a meet-the-new-neighbor's party at a 55+ condo, "Especially *Auction Bridge*."

"Did you know that millions of people play bridge worldwide in clubs, tournaments, online and with friends at home. Seniors love the game particularly. Do you play?"

"No, but tell me a little about it." his next door neighbor replied.

"Well, it seems to have started around the 1880s when the oldest known British rule book was written, although the Russian community in Constantinople played a game called <u>Solo Whist</u> and had a lot of bridge-like developments where the dealer chose the trump suite, or nominated his partner to do so. In 1904 *auction bridge* was developed in which players decide the contract through bidding, and if they make it are awarded points.

"The game became very popular when Harold Vanderbilt and others made new scoring techniques. Today, there are an estimated 25 million seniors playing it at home or in club tournaments.

"Most of the games played in America are called 'duplicate bridge'. Basically, bridge is a game of skill played with randomly dealt cards, which makes it also a game of chance, or more exactly, a tactical game with inbuilt randomness, imperfect knowledge and restricted communication, according to a definition found in the Internet's *Wikipedia*. It further states that it is a <u>mind sport</u>, and its popularity gradually became comparable to that of chess. The game has the *American Bridge League* organizing tournaments, and the *World Bridge Federation* bridge tournaments world-wide.

"Need a refill?" asked the hostess as she passed by. We both shook our heads, "No I think we have had enough."

"All right, but don't forget the hors d'oeuvres on the table."

Thanks were said, and Jerimiah went back to telling me all about bridge.

"As I was saying," he said, "Basically, you and your partner contract to make so many tricks by bidding to revealing what you have in your hand. The bidding system is a set of partnership agreements made…but I really can't simplify this procedure in a few words. It would take hours to explain the intricacies of the bidding portion of the game."

"That's what I've heard from other bridge players in our condo," the neighbor said.

"Past the bidding portion, next comes the playing to

make the tricks your bid indicated. That's another whole afternoon to cover how it works, what you have to do, etc. Bridge players love statistics, and the game produces thousands of discussions into the insight of playing. There are 128+ billion, billion, billion, billion, billion different ways to bid after the cards have been dealt. By the way, a 52-card deck is used, with four-suits (Spades, Hearts, Clubs, Diamonds) from two to Ace are dealt to the four players in a game, each ending up with 13 cards. The Ace is the highest card and a deuce the lowest, of course.

"If you have a lot of one suit in your hand you would bid it. For example, let's say you have six high spades a few high in each of the other suits you have a choice of bidding (2 spades, or you could even say 2 No Trump". That's just a simple example. By the way, 'trump" means if some one plays out a diamond and you have none, you can win the trick by trumping. Understand?"

"I've watched some bridge players in our card room so I know a little of what's happening," I countered.

"Confusing, wasn't it?"

"A little, but I get the gist of the game."

"You know we play in tournaments to obtain Master Points to obtain various titles from *Rookie* up through *Grand Life Master*, all of which provide you with some recognition to other bridge players. I've got enough points at the moment to be known as a Diamond Life Master, or 6,000 awarded points."

"That sounds like a pretty good title. What does it mean?"

"It's partly a measure of skill, but some players regard it as a measure of experience and longevity.

"I'm playing in a tournament tomorrow afternoon, why don't you come and watch for a while; you'll learn a little by watching Master Players compete.

"I might," I concluded then rising to join my wife who was talking to other condo neighbors.

The following day I went into the condo's card room. I found Jerimiah there in the far end of the room and walked over to watch. I had been watching for about an hour, when I saw Jerimiah clutch his heart area, and then collapse on the floor. Someone yelled to call 911.

After about ten minutes two men in white, wheeling a stretcher, came in and headed for the group of people at the end of the room.

After a few minutes, one of the men stood up and said, "Too late, he's dead."

They put him on the stretcher and pushed the whole contraption with Jerimiah out of the room.

I was very nervous, and very sorry that his wife was not present. But I was curious, and turned to one of the players at the table where Jerimiah had been, and asked,

"What happened?"

"You would never believe it," he replied. "It's like the Bridge of Opportunity was too much for him."

"What do you mean?"

"Do you know a little about bridge?"

"Well, Jerimiah and I had a discussion just yesterday afternoon since I didn't know the game that much."

"I'll tell you," this player said. "You know what the perfect game is in Bridge? I'll give you an example. You're dealt the 13 cards for the hand. If you get, let's say, the

Ace, King, Queen, Jack, 10, 9 and 8 of spades, three other aces with their kings…you have a hand at seven *No Trumps*, or the best one in the world out of the billions available since you take every trick. That's what he was dealt!"

"I guess that once-in-a-life opportunity was too much for Jerimiah. That gives me good reason not to learn how to play!!!"

PREDICTING

by John Ware

Gypsies do it. Magicians do it occasionally. A 'ouija' (*Weegie*) board'" attempts it. However, there is one "science" that does it from the day you were born! It's called '*biorhythms.*' <u>And its predictions have been proven to work!</u>

The name is derived from the Greek words "bios" *life*, and "rhythmos,' *a regular or measured motion*; it reflects the apparent ebb and flow of life energy.,

There are many rhythms: a physical cycle lasts 23 days long, an emotion cycle of 28 days, and a 33-day long intellectual one. On a graph they would appear as graceful curves similar to a sine wave found in information about electricity and the way currents behaved. The sine wave was like an "S" lying horizontally and backward on its side like this ᠕.

Each cycle begins when a person is born and follows the cycles it represents until the end of one's life.

There is a center horizontal line running through it, like this ──᠕. When the cycle is high there is energy to spare. On a physical high, we tend to be energetic, strong, full of vitality. On an emotional high, we are creative, artistic, aware and cheerful. On an intellectual high, we are able to think quickly and logically, and to solve complex problems.

Those highs come to the extreme point on the sixth day of these cycles where they all reach the epitome of the sine wave. However, biorhythms don't predict what will happen directly. All they do is to tell us our tendency to behave in certain ways at certain times. If we are informed about the tendency, we can usually overcome it by awareness and will power.

It was a Swiss-born businessman, George Thomnen, who brought the European science of biorhythms to the attention of the American public. He first heard of this theory while visiting his native Switzerland in the middle of the 20th century after a catastrophic head-on train wreck in which a friend of his, Han Fruch, did biorhythm graphs for the engineers and firemen on both trains, discovering that three of them were on their critical days and one on a triple low day.

Critical days are those when any of the curves cross the center or zero line; it is when our systems seem to be in flux or transition and hence unstable. Critical days are when things most likely to go wrong and people are more likely to get sick, seem to lack coordination and are therefore more accident-prone.

Scientists are still arguing over this theory. There are some that dismiss it out of hand. There are others who have proved that these life cycles can influence people with their predictive lifestyle situations.

Mr. Thomnen paid little attention to Fruch's , and others who have proved that these lifecycles can influence people. An almost identical head-on train collision later on in Pennsylvania started him wondering about the theory. He did an analysis and found out that the engineer and fireman on one train and an engineer on the other train had biorhythm charts that were extremely low on a double-critical day. He became a believer and went on to write *Is This Your Day?* that was the largest selling book in English on the subject.

It has been reported that many surgeons will perform no operations on their own critical days. Even marriage counselors are using biorhythm charts to help couples see why they get on each other's nerves and fight on certain days, with couples learning to make an extra effort to compensate for their mate's low or critical days.

The evidence on biorhythms is not all in. Clearly they are not fate, fortune-telling or predestination performers, being at most only one of the many factors which determine how we act, they are also fascinating and more than a little persuasive. As one psychologist has said, "Biorhythms are a small but significant piece of the complex puzzle of human behavior."

Recently, my wife and I were planning to fly to Europe in early July in 2002 on one of those large jumbo jets. For the fun of it, I did a biorhythm chart for both of us. Guess what. Our critical days came on the same day that our booked flight took off. We cancelled, just to protect us, and guess what?

On July 1, 2002, a major airline collided in the air with a DHL Flight cargo jet (a Boeing 757) manned by two pilots, killing all crews and passengers. P r e d i c t i o n ? Superstition?

Have you taken your Biorhythm chart yet to find

your critical days? Don't you think you should? We understand from recent research that biorhythms can affect your health.*

Check out Body Clock Information by Dr. William Shiel on MedicineNet.com and see for yourself.

CHOCOHOLIC CRAZINESS

by Hank Walton

I'm a chocoholic. A bad one, a very bad one.

I blame it on my mother. I can remember when she gave me my first tasty treat when I was about ten years old. She loved chocolate herself. When she said I was a very good son, behaved myself, hadn't gotten into too much trouble, she wanted to reward me. When giving it to me, my first piece of chocolate, she said I was going to love it the rest of my life. She was absolutely right!

Afterwards I tested many different types of chocolate, but I specifically craved for *Inalogs* that come from an area near the Swiss-Italian border.

Before I fell in love with these delicacies, I visited their factory while touring Europe. The making of this exceptional chocolate requires very special equipment and techniques.

But first, you have to go back to the beginning of chocolate to understand the whole process of why a great candy becomes an "excellent" one.

The tree from which chocolate pods are picked is from a cacao tree. It was discovered about 2,000 years ago in the tropical rain forests of the Americas. The pods of this tree contained seeds that were processed into a bitter drink by the locals in the area. The first people clearly known to have discovered the secrets of cacao were the Mayans, somewhere between 250-900 C.E. They took the tree from the rainforest and grew it in their own backyards, where they harvested, fermented, roasted and ground the seeds into a paste.

When mixed with water, chili peppers, cornmeal and other ingredients, this paste made a frothy, spicy chocolate drink. By 1400, the Aztec empire dominated a sizeable segment of Mesoamerica and traded with the Mayans and other peoples for cacao, often requiring their citizens and conquered people to pay their tribute in cacao seeds—a form of Aztec money. The drink remained bitter since sugar was an agricultural product unavailable to the ancient Mesoamericans.

In the Mayan society, many people could drink chocolate at least on occasion, although it was particularly favored by the royalty. But in the Aztec society, primarily rulers, priests, decorated soldiers, and honored merchants could partake of this sacred brew, especially during royal and religious events. Priests presented cacao seeds as offerings to the Gods and served chocolate drinks during sacred ceremonies.

During the conquest of Mexico by the Spaniards this group of conquistadors learned about chocolate, liked it, and then exported the cacao seeds back home. The Spaniards doctored up the bitter brew with cinnamon and other spices and began sweetening it with sugar.

Since the growing of cacao and processing it into a paste remained a very labor-intensive process, as was sugar, chocolate remained a very expensive import; only those with money could afford to drink it. In fact, in France, chocolate was a state monopoly that could be consumed only by members of the royal court.

For centuries this handmade luxury was sipped only by society's upper crust. However by 1880, mass production made solid chocolate candy affordable to many more people. The steam engine made it possible to drink cacao and produce large amounts of the candy cheaply and quickly. Later inventions, like the cacao press and conching machine made it possible to create smooth, creamy, solid chocolate for eating—and just a liquid chocolate for drinking.

The basic growing process of cacao in equatorial climes is the same all around the world today and farming itself remains unaltered following the traditional techniques first developed in Mesoamerica...harvesting, fermenting, drying, cleaning and roasting by hand. It's only processing by machines that have changed and brought the price down so that practically everyone can enjoy chocolate.

To make *Inalogs*, the manufacturer uses unroasted cacao beans from all over the world and are the only one who manufactures chocolate in a certain way, which sets them apart from confectioners or candy makers who make up the vast majority of companies. By controlling their batches with the top quality cacao bean, it gives the company the time to pay meticulous attention to each step and every measure of quality.

Here are the steps it takes. They carefully blend beans from a range of countries using specific flavors of each origin to create chocolate with balance and pleasing complexity. It's like a wine maker who mixes various grapes to achieve the exact taste he or she would like to sell to the public. Each piece made has a distinct profile, but all show the depth of natural flavor for which the finest cacao beans are known.

The beans are roasted by origin in small batches. Then they are blended into nibs (pieces of roasted cacao beans) from a variety of origins according to a formula in a "winnower." After this blending, the beans are ground in a "melangeur," a vintage granite mill, to make chocolate liquor. From that process, the liquor is refined with sugar and whole vanilla beans in a machine called a "concherefiner" for up to 60 hours to ensure a smooth, mellow flavor. The finished product is then made into bars and pieces for eating and further use through a tempering and molding process.

The company never cuts corners. That's what keeps INALOGs famous throughout the world. The company tells its customers that to get the full flavor of chocolate you must take a small bite and let it melt in your mouth. That's the way you'll notice the hints of fruits that makes this candy quite distinctive in the world of chocolate, and very similar to wineries throughout the world…plus they watch their quality production methods closely.

The biggest problem facing a chocoholic is that it is not only fattening when eaten in large quantities, but it can be unhealthy.

According to health articles, chocolate may support cardiovascular health, although it's unproven. Other effects include risks of cancer, coughing and heart disease…as well as causing migraines. Another reported study found chocolate consumed in great portions can cause acne and a whole other list of effects on body chemistry. Lead poisoning is another possibility.

When I found out all about these health problems, I was ready to quit. But, lo and behold, just recently I found a report that helped me keep my chocolate-loving habit in full swing.

It was found that *dark chocolate* has health benefits not seen in other varieties. It was reported in this study done at Italy's *National Institute for Food and Nutrition*, and one from the *University of Cologne* in Germany, that this type of the sweet is an antioxidant and may negate some of the pitfalls from regular varieties. There was significant drop in blood pressure, and a higher level of epicatechin, a particularly healthy compound found in chocolate.

There's nothing like being saved from doom by a bunch of research specialists throughout the world. ***Here's to chocolate, dark especially!***

The Happy Printer & Typographer

by Victor Yates

I'm in the printing business which is all about the process of reproducing text.

Prior printing methods, from the Egyptians' cursive hieroglyphs for religious literature on papyrus and wood, through the Arabic script printing press, and then the Middle Ages everything connected with printing was cumbersome.

Take for instance preparing manuscripts during the Middle Ages…all done by writing with quill and ink. All this would take hours, days, weeks, months, and sometime years to do.

Then it all started to change with moveable type that was originally created by the Chinese and Koreans and woodblock printing, and used by Gutenberg who cast his letters in metal, and added to his machine a screw-type press to stamp the inked letters against the paper.

The press was hand-operated and each piece of paper had to be placed in it one at a time. Still, the device was mechanical enough to make it cheap and efficient to print books for the masses. He managed to change the world with an already-existing technology by turning it into something that anybody could buy and use.

He was the first to mechanize printing which was a watershed event that was followed by a sea change in literacy on a global scale. It is merely an accident of history that a Bible was the first work to proliferate via the new process, it being the most popular piece in the literate civilization that survived through the Dark Ages.

While it's true that a mechanical press existed before Gutenberg, too, all he did was create a new kind of press, using mechanical presses with oil; he also used oil in his inks.

It was a long time after Gutenberg's press, that printing techniques changed. There was printing using gelatins, mimeograph, copiers and other types of reproduction techniques. The presses changed too. They were made out of metal instead of wood around 1800 with a press that used weights and counterweights. And then on to mechanized presses that used bed-and-platen technology, and those using cylinders and rotary types.

Paper use also changed. There were, of course, the sheet fed presses with individual sizes per final requirements. Then came paper on a roll invented in 1865 by William Bullock which was the first press to be fed by continuous roll paper.

Typesetting also changed. Until the late nineteenth century, all type was set and composed by hand, as in Gutenberg's workshop. Monotype and linotype machines were invented whereby operators would type on a keyboard similar to a typewriter, which produced a perforated band of paper. The band was then decoded by a machine that cast type from hot metal; these machines cast a whole row of type at a time.

A monotype machine was invented in 1889 and did basically what a linotype machine did but was used because of the advantage of being easier to correct lines of type.

Today printing techniques have been revolutionized with the use of computers. An individual using a personal computer is simultaneously doing the jobs of author, editor, and compositor.

All this is about to change. No longer will there be a "printer" or typographer. And I won't be a happy camper, nor a happy printer or typographer.

We now can talk into a computer and it then sets the type, passes it on to printing press directly…or even worse, a book is now available as an E-book. This type of book-length publication in digital form, consists of text, images, or both, and produced and published through and readable on computers or other electronic devices.

In fact, the dictionary defines the e-book as "an electronic version of a printed book."

That means I, as a printer and typographer, am basically going to be out of business. In fact, this book you are reading is only available as an e-book. The author makes more money this way…and the printer-typographer will be losing everything.

I guess that means I'm going to have to learn another type of business. I hope I'll be happy with the next one!

WHO IS THE BEST?

by Robert Weast

Do you know the best-selling copyrighted book series of all time, and the one most frequently stolen from public libraries in the United States?

I thought you said the "Bible!"

Wrong!. It is a reference book published annually, containing a collection of world records, both human achievements and the extremes of the natural world; and the book itself holds the above records all by itself.

Yep. It's *The Guinness Book of Records*. Formerly called *Guinness World Records*, and in previous U.S. editions as *The Guinness Book of World Records*. The book has become the primary international authority on the cataloging and verification of a huge number of world records.

How was it conceived? On May 4, 1951 Sir Hugh Beaver, then the managing director of the Guinness Breweries, went on a shooting party and became involved in an argument over which was the fastest game bird in Europe, the koshin golden plover or the grouse...and he realized it was impossible to confirm in reference books whether or not which bird was the correct winner.

Student twins Norris and Ross McWhirter, who had been running a fact-finding agency in London, were hired to compile what became *The Guinness Book of Records* in August 1954, with 1,000 copies printed and given away as part of a marketing give-away plan.

The first edition, published August 27, 1955, was 197 pages and went to the top of the British bestseller list by Christmas. The following year it was launched in the U.S., and it sold 70,000 copies.

Various companies owned the publication until it was finally bought by Jim Pattison Group in 2006, which is also the parent company of Ripley Entertainment.

So now there was a reference book that focused on record feats by human competitors. Such obvious things such as weight-lifting to the longest egg-tossing distance, or for the longest time spent playing Grand Theft Auto IV or the number of hot dogs that can be consumed in ten minutes, are (or were but not listed anymore) in the book.

Besides records about competitions, it contains such facts as the heaviest tumor, the most poisonous plant, the shortest river, the longest-running drama, and lots more. Many records relate to the youngest person to visit all nations of the world; all listings must be on something that will be repeated.

Every so-called record is not accepted. The list of records is constantly changing; records may be added and also removed for various reasons. The public is invited to submit applications for records, which can be either the bettering of existing records or substantial achievements which could constitute a new record.

In fact, on December 10, 2010 the publication discontinued its new "dreadlock" category after investigation of its first and only female title holder, Asha Mandela, determining it was impossible to judge this record accurately.

The latest 2013 edition has an estimated 4,000 records, and countless facts. One fact is that at least 75% of the content is brand new, i.e. a record has been broken or a new category added. There are around 1,000 photographs including new exclusive images.

The record book is about to get a new listing. I have been sitting in my bathtub full of water for the past six months because of an illness I have. The doctor said a week in the water would be good for me. After a week, I felt much better, so I decided to stay a little longer. My wife didn't like the idea, but I said eventually that I would stay in the bathtub long enough to get into the World Book of Records.

Will I make it? Get the next edition and find out!!!

THE TWEAKERS

by Charlotte Walker

There's a famous set of 137 steps in Rome where a female tourist can get her assed tweaked.

It all started in the 1950s at the Spanish Steps at a spot known as the *Via Veneto*. It's a place where a young girl could get pinched by a flirtatious Italian boy. While that kind of forward behavior has calmed down in modern times, it is still a great area of Rome…and some female tourists report back that their asses were tweaked.

The Spanish Steps were created by the French and constructed between 1723 and 1725 A.D., but the name dates back to the 18th century when the Spanish Embassy stood nearby.

Visitors to Rome have been delighted by these "Steps" since many feel they are "just stairs" from the Plaza di Spagna, which is triangular in shape, to the Villa Medici.

The steps are scenic, mysterious and elegant as they wind up a mild incline that passes through some of the most enjoyable and popular areas people love to visit in Rome. When the spring flowers are erupting all over

Rome, the Spanish Steps are alive with the sight and smell of azaleas that pour over from the many greenhouse along the walk.

The spring weather in Rome turns hot after this burst of flowers which have announced the beginning of summer, even into the autumn months.

There are many cafes, shops and restaurants near the Spanish Steps that are always popular in warm weather. Many people enjoy taking a snack or light lunch and just resting on the steps themselves and enjoying the sights as they dine.

When you reach the bottom of the stairs you will find another of the many great outdoor art pieces by Bernini called the *La Barcaccia Fountain* (or the Fountain of the Old Boat). The ship that is the centerpiece of this stunning fountain might have been designed by the artist's son. It was built in 1627 under the commission of Pope Urbano VIII Barberini. The water from this fanciful fountain literally pours from the artistic "leaks" in the hull of the ship.

The steps are not designed to be an athletic challenge so there are three big flattened parts of the steps where you can take time to catch your breath and maybe have a bite to eat.

There are many things to see around the Step area, and any travel agent can list them for you before visiting the area.

But it is the ass tweaking thing we are concerned about.

After a terrible amount of research we found out that there really is a school to learn *ass tweaking*. Teen age boys, and even those much older, can pay a tutor for a week of learning how to tweak asses.

It is not a simple procedure because it must be conducted without being noticed, with the proper amount of learning how to squeeze, and exactly what part of the ass should be violated. Some boys must actually take the course over because they do not learn the right technique in a one-week course.

From what we can learn, the tweaking business is a very private affair and there are very few people who want to talk about the right place to tweak a girl's butt.

One thing we did learn. The girls in Italy know all about getting the right butt exercise to get the best one for boys to do the tweaking. Checking out the Internet, we found that one's body has a number of ways and exercises that are important to create the perfect ass....some for tightening and some for making it bigger, calisthenics to use, foods to avoid when trying to tighten and tone it, exercises to use in bed, to make a muscular one, making a flat butt round...and at least over 50 more ideas to help achieve the perfect ass for tweakers to work on.

You laugh. But to some people a perfect butt to help find the husband of your future is important in Italy, and probably lots of other places on the earth.

One story came from the mouth of one of the teachers in this ass class that was dominated by very young men. It was the time a girl applied and was accepted into the class.

It seems that the modern girl today is a little more aggressive, and they too would like to tweak the best ass that can be found. It seems that the ass is a very important part of the body when it comes to sexual satisfaction.

Who knew?

THE TRAVELERRRRR

by Bruce Brown

Hello.

I'm an earthy element.

My name is not important.

But I've been around the world, traveling.

I've been to many places, and am still going all over the world.

Let me explain.

I was born many years ago and have a lot of cousins who also travel with me. My parents may have been brought here by my grandparents. I'm not sure; however, that's not important.

I'm here, and here to stay.

And I do get to travel a great deal, just like I told you.

I've been to mountain tops.

I've been to valleys.

I've been to the oceans.

I've been all over the earth, in various modes.

You, my dear reader, you always need me when you travel.

I'm occupationally employed all the time and don't collect unemployment insurance.

At times you can't find me.

But, you need me as your most important friend

Sometimes I hide in different disguises.

Sometimes I'm around and you don't want me.

I don't feel neglected, in that case, just a little embarrassed that you try to get rid of me and send me other places.

I know you really don't mean it, but such is life.

I've been known to transfer my image so that people can love me, or hate me.

I have many modes of travel. On the ground, in the ocean, in the air. You name it, I'm probably involved.

At times I can annoy you. At times you love me!

I mix well with a lot of things, and some things I can't although I try real hard.

I do leave an impression wherever I go on land.

I've been called a destroyer. I've been called a healer.

Besides humans loving me, other species and things do too!

I've been used to do a lot of things. But, hey, that's what I'm occupied with and keeps me employed all of the time.

I've been known to disappear, and when I do everybody hates me. When I come back, they heartily embrace me. That's the kind of personality I have.

I have outstanding qualities, however, that can be measured, examined, identified...you know, all the good ones. I do have some very bad ones when I get angry, and you've met them too.

I've been known to go on long trips for years, centuries,

millenniums. When I return, I'm welcomed with open arms. That gives me a nice feeling.

I can change my looks whenever the weather permits it. You always find me no matter what I do.

It's great to feel "loved".

I have been "unloved" as well.

Unfortunately, there is nothing that either you or I can do about it.

My parents and grandparents love to talk about me all the time. Sometimes they show pictures, too.

My name, in case you haven't figured it out is…..

H2o.

Hello there!

I'll be running along since some of my cousins are looking for me, including: aqueducts, aquifers, artesian wells, bedrock, condensation, drainage basins, erosion, evaporation, floods, fresh water, geysers, glaciers, ground water, headwaters, hydroelectric dams, hurricanes, icebergs, mining water, oceans, portables, rain, reservoirs, runoffs, saline water, septic tanks, sewage treatment plants, snow, springs, streams, tornadoes, tributaries, watersheds, weather, wells.

See ya around.

KEEP THE LIGHTS BURNING

by Jean Maly

After my mother passed away, I was the responsible family member who had to clean up her apartment, divide all the knick knacks and furniture among the rest of the descendants and those who didn't want anything, and also arrange for a "garage sale" to get rid of the balance.

Among some surprising "thanks, but I don't want anything" was my grandmother's candlesticks that my mother had inherited years ago from her mother. They were now a tarnished pair of golden sticks which appealed to no one.

Before taking and putting them into the sale, I tried to clean them up as much as possible. At least, I thought, they were now more saleable.

I advertised in the local newspaper under "Garage Sales" for one week-end toward the end of the year since I thought that would be the perfect time to sell the over 100 pieces available.

The Saturday morning before the sale culminated weeks of gathering and marking prices for each item, without any help from anyone in the family, I was prepared for the sale.

I had priced the candlesticks pretty high because I thought they were valuable enough to get a good price for them. I even displayed them prominently up front in my garage hopefully to draw attention to these wonderful candlesticks. I can remember my mother praying over them. I didn't want them since I had already bought a pair when I visited the land of Israel years before.

It was towards the end of Sunday, the last day of the sale, that anyone really showed any interest in the candlesticks. It was a little old lady who looked like she was suffering from a lot of old-age diseases.

She picked up the candlesticks, looked them over, and brought them to me and asked. "Is this the best price you can do?"

"Yes," I replied, "But if you are really interested in buying them, make me a decent offer."

"I should," she replied, "Since they remind me of the ones I had in my family before they were lost in World War II. I know some of my family escaped to America before the war started and brought with them all their valuables…the candlesticks were not among them."

She asked me my name.

I told her, "Shirley Rosencrantz.", which was my maiden name and one I used again after divorcing my husband of twenty-five years.

"That's interesting," she promptly said, "My last name is the same as yours."

"Well, that is a coincidence. Where did your family come from, Europe?"

"Yes. They came over when I was a little girl. They,

too, escaped with whatever valuables they could. The candlesticks they had were not one of the items they took. When I saw yours which looked exactly the same they had left, I was intrigued but they are a little more than I can afford to spend."

"What town did your family live in," I inquired.

" A small village in Poland called Postankisk."

"Oh, my," I countered. "That's where my family lived, too. What street did you live on?"

" Pilingsberg"

"Oh my gosh. They did, too. What number?"

"202."

"For heavens sake. They lived at 204 and must have been next door neighbors."

"You're right. Now that I look at you closely, you look just like your mother a little bit. What a coincidence."

"No," I said, "It's fate. Those candlesticks were waiting for you to claim them all the time. By coincidence you came across them with the family that lived next door to you. I would love you to have them."

"I would love them, and would like to meet with you some more under better circumstances so we can discuss our backgrounds, people your family must have known, and much more. Would you like that?"

"Of course," I said as I handed over the candlesticks to her. "You can have them at no cost."

"I couldn't. Can I pay you a little?"

"Absolutely not. I would be most honored to have a former next door neighbor to my family have these candlesticks so you can keep the candles burning during the rest of your life. I'm sure my mother would be pleased, Ms. Rosencrantz."

"Well thank you, too, Ms. Rosencrantz. I would love to keep the candles burning every Friday night, and will say the usual Sabbath prayers over them, plus at least a million more for your courtesy."

"One or two I wouldn't mind," I replied. "Hope we can meet soon to talk more."

THE HIT OF THE SHOW

by Jerome Light

The wedding invitations were sent. Plans were finalized through the wedding planner.

During the ceremony my fiancée and I decided to have three married members in attendance give a short talk about marriage. One were newly married, the next were married 20 years, and the third couple were my grandparents who were married almost 63 years (62 and three quarters, actually!). We told each couple to send us a copy before the wedding to make sure there were no conflicts in the talks which we were sure would be one of the hits of the show (ceremony).

The day of the wedding arrived. It was a beautiful day. The wedding rehearsal the day before had been a little confusing but everything was straightened out at the end of two hours.

More than 175 attendees straggled in to find seats before the wedding started. Fortunately, everything went according to the wedding-planner's plans.

We got to the portion when the married couples were going to give their little speech about marriage. The first two speeches were exactly as the copies they had sent to us a few months before..

The grandparent's speech was a little changed, and we are going to include it in its entirety here. This is what they said:

"We were married on November 6, 1949…or 62-3/4 years ago.

"You ask how come so long? We attribute this longevity to many things…A good heritage, good doctors, Medicare, Social Security, successful treatments, good nutrition, exercise via physical and mental routines, and a bunch of vitamins we consume each day thrown in for good measure.

"Plus a marriage philosophy that includes not too much aggravation over the little things, the ability to survive the traumas of life while keeping our "YES DEAR" outlook to make each other happy under trying circumstances…and being there when needed…and an occasional glass of wine.

"But most important…we are still in LOVE with each other after almost 63 years of marriage, and with the ability to continue to please each other no matter what.

"And especially…we always kiss before going to sleep each night no matter what!!

"We wish the same to our grandson and his new partner in life. May you enjoy the same experiences we have had through the rest of your lives…and don't forget…kiss each other before going to sleep each night of your marriage

We wish the newlyweds a long and happy life together… and close by using a quote which appeared in the December 1983 Reader's digest—YOU DON'T MARRY ONE PERSON…YOU MARRY THREE…the person you think they are, the person they are, and the person they are going to become as the result of being married..

"With a great deal of LOVE…G & G

"P.S. Grandma says…it is not necessary to always have the last word…sometimes. Silence is golden…sometimes… Just remember, a certain look will do the trick."

At the reception held right after the wedding I saw many guests going over to my grandparents, apparently thanking them for giving their remarks.

Later on, my grandparents walked over to us at the head table and told of all the complimentary remarks they had received from wedding guests for their dissertation on a long-married life.

It was my grandfather who surprised me. "I tell you grandson, I never had such enjoyment of being part of the wedding. It was like an actor on the stage. I thoroughly enjoyed it. In fact, I would like to go on the stage more often. I did it when I was younger, and did some acting for a local dramatic club. In fact, I played a tomato at the 1939 World's Fair in New York City. It was fun."

You know what happened a few weeks later. I received a call from my grandfather who said, "Grandson, you won't believe what I did. I went to a local dramatic club call for actors and I was accepted for the grandfather's role in a play. It's like a dream come true!!!

21 Gone Awry

By Paul Glatz

The card game, Blackjack, also known as "21" is very popular in the casinos of the world. It was conceived not too long ago.

Playing cards are believed to have been invented in China or India around 900 A.D. The Chinese are thought to have originated card games when they began shuffling paper money, which was another Chinese invention, into various combinations. In China today, the term for playing cards means "paper tickets."

The 52-card deck used now was originally called the "French Pack" which derived its name around the 1600s from the French games "chemin de fer" and "French Ferme. While very popular in ancient Greece, though illegal, gambling has been part of the human experience ever since.

Blackjack originated in French casinos about 1700 where it was called "vingi-et-un" or "twenty and one." It has been played in the U.S. since the 1800s. The name derived its nomenclature because if a player got a Jack of Spades and an Ace of Spades as the first two cards dealt to him (one up and one face down) he or she received additional money in the payoff. In casinos today, any combination of the first two cards the player is dealt adding to "21" no matter if the cards are in hearts, diamonds, clubs of spades, or a mixture of suits, it's called "Blackjack" by the dealer and the player receives a three-two payoff (if you bet $10, you receive $15) immediately rather than even money from the total bet before the deal.

Gambling was legalized in the Western United States from the 1850s to around 1910 at which time the state of Nevada made it a felony to operate a gambling game. However, in 1911, Nevada re-legalized casino gambling where Blackjack became one of the primary games of chance offered to gamblers. Atlantic City followed, and right now there are many Indian tribes running casinos in their state where Blackjack is played alongside slot machines.

There have been many efforts to apply mathematics to the game. Pioneers in this attempt used calculators, probability and statistic theories to substantially reduce the "house" advantage. After the computer came along, it was much easier to help the gambler win. Today, the odds are just about even for the house and the player. That's why the game is so popular.

Other meanings of "21" have arisen, too. For instance, in mathematics its proper divisors are 1,3,7. Adding up the sums for the numbers 1 through 6 yields 21. In science, it is the atomic number for scandium. In astronomy the number connotes a barred spiral galaxy in the constellation Andromeda.

Here a few other things about the number 21.

Twenty-one has been the legal age of adulthood in

many countries around the world, before it was lowered to 18 in the United States. The number is the legal age at which one can purchase an alcohol drink, with a few exceptions in certain counties of a U.S. state. It is also the legal age to gamble and work as a prostitute in Nevada. In most states a person must be over 21 to rent a car.

In sports, 21 is a variation of street basketball in which each player (there can be any number) plays for himself only in making the requisite number of baskets.

In other fields, the current years 2001 to 2100 is referred to as the 21st Century. This inspired a number of companies to include the number 21 in their corporate names—Century 21 Real Estate and Century 21 Television to name a notable two.

Here are other interesting facts about the number.

The number of spots on a standard cubicle die in a pair of dice is 1+2+3+4+5+6…which adds up to 21.

The number of firings in a gun salute to Royalty or leaders of countries…usually is called a 21-Gun Salute.

It was the title of a Quiz Show that ran from 1956 to 1958, and most remembered for the scandal that was associated with it.

Is there anything else about Blackjack you should know?

The <u>TWIST</u> to this story can be found in a book published by a company called "KARANDELL CORP." To learn about how Blackjack and 21 fit into this fictionalized story, send an e-mail to karandell@juno. com, and they will forward a way for you to get an answer of how 21 has gone awry!

WHO YOU GONNA CALL

by Audrey Blacke

Many years ago I had a terrible problem. Something to do with my family.

I needed help from a government agency. I turned to the telephone book and tried to find the necessary help agency among all the government listings.

Nothing. No "help" classifications number one. Number two, the type in the phone book must have been six point and very hard to read.

I made some calls to some well-known disease associations, but still couldn't find my helper.

Finally, after two days of search I found the agency that could help me.

After this episode was all over, I told my sad story to my husband, an editor-publisher of many magazines during his lifetime.

"Honey," I said, "Listen to my sad story of looking for help from a governmental agency."

"Really?" he replied, "Show me what you did."

So I went to the phone directory that was given to me by our local telephone company and showed him the listings I went to, the small type (we had to use a magnifying glass to be able to read the listings) the telephone company used to list their clients.

"Yep," he said, "It's difficult to find what you are looking for, and the type is too small."

"There's got to be a better way for people to get help," I concluded. "Maybe you can think of something."

"I'll think about it," my husband commented, "Give me a couple of days.

"I pondered your problem and actually went through the same procedure you did to get the feel of the problem," my husband started to talk to me at dinner a few days later.

"Here's what I propose.

"The first thing to do is that we have to increase the size of the type we have to read…which I've done on a dummy I've made.

"The second thing was to reorganize our thinking and coming up with a solution. I examined all the things that affect our senior lifestyle, put them down on paper, and when finished put them in alphabetical order.

"For instance, the following things may affect us at one time or another…Abuse, Automobiles, Blood, Civil Rights, Consumer Affairs, Courts, Credit, Crime, and so forth. It came to about 108 different categories that affect our life- styles.

"Other headings included doctors, education, elderly, emergencies, enforcement, food and drugs, fraud, housing, legal, Medicare and Medicaid, marriage, postal, property, sexual, Social Security, taxes, traffic, transportation, voting, water…and another 50 headings I haven't mentioned.

"I placed these headings in alphabetical order to make it easier for searchers to find help quickly.

"I put a description of exactly what was included on the front cover : 'Handy, Quick-Find PHONE DIRECTORY & SOURCE GUIDE of Where-to-Call for HELP from LOCAL-COUNTY-STATE-FEDERAL GOVERNMENTAL ORGANIZA-ZATIONS, & LIFELINE-LIFESTYLE GROUPS.

I loved it. My husband made thousands of copies to give to friends, and vendors who want to use it as a promotional tool to their customers

"HELP PHONE DIGEST is being distributed by various vendors in the three South Florida counties in separate editions.

If you wish a FREE copy, e-mail a request to Karandell@juno.com and you'll learn how to get one… *and know who you gonna call when you need "Help."*

WHERE'S MY MONEY GONE

by Sylvan Grossman

Like most of the world, I like "money."

I never researched how it was started until recently because I was curious…and I was going to write a story about it for this book.

According to my best reference on the Internet, Wikipedia, money is described as any object or record that is generally accepted as payment for goods and services and repayment of debts in a given socio-economic context or country.

The money supply of a country consists of currency (banknotes and coins) and bank money (the balance held in checking and savings accounts). Bank money usually forms by far the largest part of the money supply.

Barter methods were probably the first used to pay for service or products. Eventually commodity money was used, and the first usage of "money" came from Mesopotamia around 3000 BC.

The word "money" is believed to originate from a temple of Hera, located on Capitoline, one of Rome's seven hills.

In the past, money was generally considered to have the following main functions: *medium of exchange, unit of account,* and *store of value.*

When money is used to intermediate the exchange of goods and services, it is performing a *medium of exchange* and thereby avoids the inefficiencies of a barter system.

Unit of account is a standard numerical unit of measurement of the market value of goods, services, and other transactions; it is also known as a "measure" or "standard" of relative worth and deferred payment which may be divisible into smaller units without loss of value.

To act as a *store of value,* money must be able to be reliably saved, stored and retrieved—and be predictably usable as a medium of exchange when it is retrieved.

Money acts as a standard measure and common denomination of trade; it is a basis for quoting and bargaining of prices.

Currently, most modern monetary systems are based on fiat money; however, for most of history almost all money was commodity money, such as gold and silver coins.

Commercial bank money or demand deposits are claims against financial institutions that can be used for the purchase of goods and services.

When gold and silver are used as money, supply can grow only if these metals are increased by mining. However, modern day monetary systems are no longer tied to the value of gold.

Governments and central banks have taken both regulatory and free market approaches to monetary policy. Some of the tools used are changing the interest rate at which the central bank loans money to borrowers and the commercial banks. There are other effects that influence monetarism that we will not discuss here.

One thing we do know. Problems with currency in other countries can influence our money values. That and the governments printing as much money as they wish without precious metal backing it can cause inflation and other problems.

The most important thing occuring with money is what happens to me. If I take out $100 in cash from the bank, I'll use it up in about three months…because most everything I buy today is put on a charge card whose monthly sum I'm bound to pay with a paper check that is backed up with the amount of money I have in my checking account. I can pay off that debt by writing a check for the full amount, or pay part down and pay interest on the balance by "technically borrowing" cash from the credit card companies.

That's the twist about money. If you have a lot of it, you don't have to worry. If you have to pay interest on what you don't pay for your credit charges, it can cost you a lot more than you thought. If you remember the very fourth story in this publication called "Creditworthy", there are a lot of people using their money this way (deferred payment).

Another way we now use money is by paying our owed debts on-line with a computer. What we do is save time and save the postage required to send a check; we rarely, if ever, send cash to pay a bill.

Then there is the procedure of having a bill paid automatically from your bank account on a scheduled basis….and have your money deposited electronically into your account, just as the Social Security Administration is going to be doing for everyone very soon.

I predict that money will disappear from existence in the not-too-distant future. It will be the same feeling as when robots replace the human workers. Everybody will be doing it so you won't be "different!"

That's when I can ask..."Where Has My Money Gone?"

A Fireman Is Not
Always A "Fireman"

by Spartan Lane

I just saw a city housing complex burn almost to the ground.

The best thing I heard was that no one was killed or burned beyond recognition.

This entire city block in my hometown was burning throughout the day, but not a single fire truck was spotted rushing to the scene.

That's because more than 250 firefighters from across the country and one from overseas were already at the site setting the blazes themselves.

The rescue workers were participating in a three-day fire training program hosted by the local Firefighters Benevolent Association.

I learned that this particular city housing complex was scheduled to be demolished later in the month, so it gave firemen a chance to go inside of a real building that's on fire for training, something that is very hard to find.

Officials spent nearly a week preparing the buildings that were built in the late 1950s, including removing asbestos and other things that may pose a hazard during fire-training..

Teams took turns igniting the 24-unit complex, crawling into the raging blazes and extinguishing them. Some practiced using industrial saws to crack open roofs, while others sharpened their skills on breaking down doors and smashing windows.

One of the participants and I had a long talk about this special operation. "More than anything, the real value is making new friends and learning from everyone else; we all share the same passion of the profession that calls for saving people's lives."

Participants pay to take part in the training and all proceeds benefit the local Firefighters' Sick and Injured Fund. The training director told me that the complex should have been destroyed years ago.

I did find out, however, that a *fireman* is not always a "man" since women have joined many fire departments.

I also learned that the word "fireman" can be defined for other things than just an individual employed to extinguish fires and rescue people (and animals, too.)

A "fireman" can be an individual employed to tend the fire for running a steam engine, either on a stationary engine, or a railway locomotive or a steamship.

The United States Navy has a rate for an enlisted seaman who works on ships' propulsion systems, even though steamships are no longer used.

A "fireman" can also be a baseball player who enters the game after the starting pitcher is removed.

Also, a fireman can be a pyromaniac or arsonist. In the entertainment field, an individual employed to start fires to burn books is called one in the novel *Fahrenheit*

451. There also have been many motion pictures using the word, too.

This word "fireman" is known as a *disambiguation*, would you believe? A page in an encyclopedia lists articles associated with the same title, as we explained above.

Disambiguation. There's a new twist to the English language! You'd better be sure that the link you are led to goes directly to the intended article you wanted. Otherwise, you have been *disambigulated*!

!

No Drought About It

by Carl Kirschen

Researchers have gone back to the Mayan civilization to find that the weather and climate change was responsible for its disintegration.

What they found was famine, war and collapse as a long-term wet weather pattern shifted to drought.

An international research team compiled a detailed climate record that tracked 2,000 years of wet and dry weather in present day Belize, where Maya cities developed from the year 300 to 1000. Data trapped in stalagmites (mineral deposits left by dripping water in caves) as well as using the rich archaeological evidence created by the Mayans, backed up the findings.

Unlike our current global warming trend which is reportedly spurred by human activities, including the emission of atmosphere-heating greenhouses gases, the Maya collapse was due to a massive, undulating natural weather pattern.

The pattern brought extreme moisture, which fostered the growth of the Maya civilization, and periods of dry weather and drought on a centuries-long scale. The wet periods meant expanded agriculture and growing population as Maya centers of civilization flourished. It also reinforced the power of the kings of these centers, who claimed credit for the rains that brought prosperity and performed public blood sacrifices meant to keep the weather favorable to farming.

After the rainy period changed to dry weather, the king's powers and influence collapsed and paralleled closely with an increase in wars over scarce resources.

The collapse started around 900 when prolonged drought undermined their authority; however, Maya populations remained for about another century until a severe drought which lasted 100 years forced them to leave their biggest centers of population.

Even during the height of their power, humans had an impact on their environment, mostly farming more land which in turn caused greater erosions. During the dry period, the Maya farmers responded with intensified plantings.

When the climate shifted toward drought, in a long-running pattern called the inter-tropical conversion zone, it inflamed human impact on the environment.

This story has a twisted funny ending because there are some similarities to this in the modern context that we need to worry about…such as in Europe and Africa.

If there are changes in climate that undermine agricultural systems to some areas, it could create wide-spread famine, social unrest and warfare that then draw in other populations, just as it may have happened in the Maya civilization. There were famines in Russia, North Korea, Bengal, Somalia, United States, Ireland, Medieval

Europe, India, Laois, Australia to name some areas over the past few hundred years.

When examining the patterns, there is a very similar one going on around the world that should make a great world famine possible.

Should we worry? Absolutely, say many researchers who make it their business to examine the impact on weather conditions throughout the world.

Be prepared, especially this year when the drought in the United States, a country that has been at war for quite a number of years, had one of the worst droughts in years forcing corn food prices to rise, cattle killed and other crops suffering.

These coincidences make you worry that *There's No Drought About It!*

A REALLY SHORT, SHORT-STORY

by Bernard Block

Short stories in this Omnibus-1 are a form of short fictional narrative prose. Short stories tend to be more concise and to the point than longer works of fiction, such as novellas and novels. Because of their brevity, successful ones rely on literary devices such as character, plot, theme, language, and insight to a greater extent than long-form fiction.

One of the things that intrigued us as we formulated this book, how long does a short-story have to be within our definition. We picked 500-2000 as our range. Some are shorter, some are longer, but not by much.

We do have a challenge for you, however. Can you write a short story shorter than the one shown on the next page. If you can, there's a reward for you. Check what we have written for our very short story.....

Our very, very short story.......

I Came, Saw, Conquered!

That's it. These seven words and punctuations tell a complete story, we think. We would like to hear from you and receive your copy of a short, short-story which we will publish in our next edition of <u>The Short, Short-Story Omnibus-2,</u> if we like it. ...and also send you a copy of our first publication our company released...*The Sleeping Girl on the Couch*, by this writer. **NOTE: *The first chapter of this book is included after this page and used as a short story!***

Plus, you will receive a share of the proceeds with other published authors in this edition, after costs from all sales of this E-Book have been taken (Around $1000)

For more details, call 1-561-638-9090.

THE SLEEPING GIRL ON THE COUCH

by Bernard Block

The nude woman lay there, on the couch.

Exquisite.

Her long hair flowed toward the right side of her body, framing a love face. Full lips, eyes closed.

Her breasts, flushed back against her body, cast a shadow downward across her abdomen as the spotlights on the high ceiling above poured forth their illuminating rays.

The artist had captured this majestic moment perfectly through a three-dimensional, all-white paper bas-relief which was mounted on a pure white muslin fabric, with the whole thing ensconced in a clear Lucite case. It all added up to a pure, serene scene of a work of art that "hit me" as I strolled through the two-story art gallery on a major street near where I work and live.

"I must have it," I murmured to myself, "It's absolutely perfect."

But would my wife Andrea, talking to Rita Barone, the owner of the gallery, like such a lovely in our home we planned to move into shortly?" Not that I was henpecked. I was so much in love with her after all these years of marriage that most of our purchases, art or otherwise, were done on a "we both like it basis" and "let's please each other" rather than fighting over an incidental thing, or an interfering ego, or whatever seems to have sent a lot of married couples to the divorce wars.

"Art" had entered our lives innocently. We needed it for wall decorations, or we must bring back something while on a vacation, or even through impulse.

There was the time we were wending our way through a local department store and simultaneously spotted a bronze statue of a nude man and woman tenderly embraced in each other's arms. We both looked at one another and said let's buy it for our anniversary, which we did. It now stands on a dresser in our bedroom.

Or the time we were traveling in California on a second honeymoon just after our twentieth wedding anniversary celebration. While browsing through the famous San Francisco specialty store, *Gumps*, we saw this bronze statue of a young boy running with a string of multi-colored balloons in his hands that bobbed up and down when you touched them. We spent more money on that one piece of "art" than on our airline tickets to get us there. It was a memento that helped us remember our visit to the west coast of the United States and that scintillating city every time we looked at this sculpture which sits on a **cocktail table in our living room.**

But this. This lovely, sleeping, nude woman on a couch hanging on walls in other homes, or in galleries to be sold, as well as in museum exhibitions. Lovely ladies of white paper. Inviting? No, not inviting. She was at peace.

Here was the most pleasurable female I had ever seen captured by an artist. Sexually exciting through my own fantasy-like dreams, especially when I could awake her from the sleeping spell. Yet really serene in a pose the artist had placed her to portray his theme for the title of the work...*THE SLEEPING GIRL ON THE COUCH.* He had used the bas-relief method which was a technique using white mulched paper placed over a solid sculpture base to form the finished artwork.

The material the artist used—mulched white paper—added to the overall feeling of this piece of "art." I learned from vivacious gallery owner, Rita Barone, how it was produced.

"The special white paper is mulched to a certain consistency and then laid over a cast statue to reproduce the copies created for sale. These are not mass produced copies by an automatic press," she said. "Everything is done by hand. Probably more than half of the pieces produced are redone since they don't meet the artist's exacting requirements. They are so good, even the local art museum has bought one for its permanent collection."

I found out the artist, Ted Glatz, was fussy. Rita explained that she had a long talk with him when he visited her earlier in the year and learned all about his art and production method for this particular piece. She had purchased two of them for sale.

Once again I said to myself. I must have it.

The price?

"$2,000," Rita advised.

It didn't phase me even if it would be the most expensive piece of "art" I ever bought. I'm not wealthy, just a middle class advertising executive in an ad agency.

I couldn't understand why I fell in love with the woman in white. Even days later, after my wife had seen it and said she too thought it was a wonderful piece, commented that if I liked it we should buy it, although being practical, added, "It's a lot more than we normal pay for art!"

$2,000. I heard the price, but it didn't seem to bother me. I wanted that piece of "art" very badly. Did I want that serene nude beauty in white to admire...to touch? Was I getting a middle-age syndrome?" To have a young girl? To taste her all over? To feel the taut skin? To admire a perfect face, a soft, yet firm breast? To vicariously overcome my middle-class inhibitions?

Why was I falling in love with this closed-eyed, cast-paper beauty?

Or was it the captured moment the artist portrayed? The innocence of the scene? Whatever, it was magnificent. Glatz had reached me far more than any other thing I had seen in museums, galleries, stores.

Even better than the great masters?

I guess so. An older man dreams a lot.

"$2,000. I would have to scrape from many places to raise the money. But it was worth it and this piece of "art" would be the centerpiece in the new home we were going to move into shortly.

A few days later I told Andrea to tell gallery-owner Rita Barone, whom she new quite well while working at the local art museum, "we'll take it."

"You are lucky," Rita told Andrea who called her later the same day. "The price has gone up $500, but you can have it at the old price."

What did I care, I thought, when she told me about

the rise in price and the amount of the first-quoted price we would have to pay, $2,000.

I did not buy my sleeping lady for an investment.

I bought her to admire, to dream, to love.

Little did I realize what would happen to my dreams.

(To get the rest of the story, e-mail karandell@juno.com)

MODELING AROUND

by Jacob Truvay

"Let me tell you about what happened with my daughter and the modeling business," said my next door neighbor George while we were taking a rest from watering our lawns.

"Even though you have a great looking face and body and want to get into the modeling business, you need the smarts to break into it. You have to realize that chances of becoming the sort of super model who lands multi-million dollar endorsements are only a little better than chances of being killed by a charging tiger—even if you are beautiful.

"The success stories are few. Even models represented by the best agencies in the world often take other work to supplement their income."

I took a gulp of water from my thermos while he continued on his soliloquy.

"There are many different kinds of models as you might know—child models, plus-size models, parts models for hands you might see in diamond ring ads, and, of course, the fashion ones. Fashion models must usually conform to a rather rigid physical criteria, but there are others called 'real life' models who are often also actors,. They are just what the name implies: ordinary-looking people used in catalogs and commercials to represent someone the average consumer can identify with easily. I remember reading that the white-haired guy with the pot belly on golf course resort billboards is a real-life model. If it turns out you aren't quite what advertisers need in a fashion model, most unsuccessful models look for this kind of work since it is like being a character actor in a movie.

"The model who gets all the attention, of course, is the cat-walking high-fashion one. Do you know that for those types of models you have to start somewhere between 15 to 17 years of age, though probably closer to 15. Agencies tend to want to invest their time in someone young because models' careers don't last as long as physicians, so you have to start training early. Models should be tall, long-legged and lean; the minimum model's body should be about 5'8" high, have an average weight of 108 to 125 pounds and preferably be one with small breasts. These characteristics are partly aesthetic and partly practical because this type of frame looks good on the runway and in front of the cameras which, they say, adds 15 pounds. A scrawny build drapes clothing nicely and ensures a good fit in the standard wardrobe. There are always exceptions to the rule, but generally the closer you are to the industry norm, the better your chances.

"A candidate for becoming a male model can start a little later, roughly between the ages of 18 to 21 since the industry doesn't want a male model to look too childish. A man's modeling career usually lasts longer than a woman's, and since ten-year old boys more often would rather be playing sports or blowing up things than strutting down a runway, this side of the business tends to be less competitive as well. The average dimensions for a male model are a height of 5'11" to 6'2" and a weight of 140-165 pounds. The male model should be fit, not bulging with muscles, but definitely healthy. All models…"

Suddenly his cell phone rang and he took it out of the jeans he was wearing. He put up his hand to let me know he had to take the call, and then walked away. After a few minutes he returned and picked up where he left off on his story about modeling.

"As I was saying. All models work through an agent usually, although there are some who freelance. An agent is responsible for obtaining bookings and making sure a model shows up on time, no matter how sick, or hung over or down-in-the-dumps. Most agents, if they are good, will advise models about clothes and hair, and generally guide through the various stages of their career.

"It's not easy to find an agent. A striking girl may be walking in a street, in an airport, anywhere, when an agent from a reliable agency may spot her, recognize her potential, and give her a business card. Unfortunately, this is a rare occurrence.

"There are modeling agencies that often open their doors to hundreds of local hopefuls through what is known in the business as an '*open call*.' There a lot of competitors during this process, and it normally takes a long time for the waiting pros inside to size you up and consider what might be your potential. Guaranteed there are more rejections in this procedure, but at least they are 'free' for an individual to attend. Agencies usually advise not to waste your money on professional photos. Just bring a few informal snapshots, full body ones and some from the side are advised, one nice head shot, and a casual clothed shot.

"However, a model-to-be doesn't have to wait around for an *open call*. They can always go around to agencies without waiting for one. Wanna-be models must beware of those who charge an exorbitant entry fee to look you over at model-search contests."

My neighbor stopped his story and asked if I wanted to hear more about the modeling business. I said yes.

He continued. "There is another option to get into the modeling business, although it does not occur that often. Attend a modeling convention. Entry fees are usually high, but you get the opportunity to meet representatives from several different agencies all at the same time, and a chance to learn more about the industry. There are even well-respected service agencies on the Internet which give you an opportunity to post an electronic profile so that the pros can check you out.

"If an agency decides you are model material, an agent will arrange to have portfolio pictures taken, a composite card printed, and a resume put together. In the portfolio you bring to job interviews, called '*go-sees*,' there should be a series of shots taken by an agency-recommended photographer that reflects the agency's marketing strategy for you. Yes, agencies have marketing strategies strange as it may seem. Composite cards, called '*comp cards*' are what you leave behind with prospective employers, usually a single sheet of photos to help them remember you.

"There's more to the modeling business you might want to know. There are really two modeling industries, the legitimate one that pays models a fair price for their services, and the scam one which preys on young wanna-be models suckering as much money possible out of such prospects.

"There are photographers who try to sell expensive portfolio shots before approaching agencies… that's a common one….telling prospects they will never get anywhere unless they have a professional presentation. It's better just to have snapshots, and if the agency likes those they will help you arrange all the portfolio photographs you'll need.

"There is another scam you have to watch out for; it's called 'Fly-by-Night' agencies that charge registration fees, and are mostly trying to get potential models to pay for expensive portfolios then finding them work. When approaching such an outfit make sure they have been around for a while, have a nice big ad in the Yellow Pages, and check with the Better Business Bureau to see if there have been any complaints made against them.

"Here's another scam that's part of the business, the so-called 'Modeling Schools.' Some say it's a good way to get some experience, as long as there is money to burn. Don't worry, the modeling business does not require any schooling to get into this line of work and become successful at it."

George stopped again to get a drink of water, then started once again to talk about modeling. "One last thing, flattery and high pressure tactics are all signs of a con artist operation. When asked to pose naked or to have sex in exchange for jobs, you'll know you have met a 'sleazeball' looking out for no one but himself and trying to have fun."

Once again George paused to take a brief rest. "I didn't realize I had so much to say about this part of the 'art' business, but I learned an awful lot when my daughter tried.

"Another thing I learned was that you should tell a model wanna-be to head straight for New York City. It's the U.S. jump-off point for the modeling world, and most super models live in that city for at least part of the year. Of course, a couple of years modeling in Miami or Los Angeles won't hurt a career. Hard work, connections and luck all play a part in where you end up. There is still a demand for models in secondary markets such as Chicago, Philadelphia and Phoenix.

"My one last comment about the modeling business. Always have a sharp, dependable lawyer you can count on to look over contracts and anything else you may have to sign."

Figuring he had finished, I queried, "What happened to your daughter?"

"You won't believe it! She met a male model on her very first job and they both fell in love with each other. They dated two times and found out they had great personal similarities, so they eloped to Vegas and got married. It didn't take long for her to get pregnant, so that ended her search to get into modeling.

"But I'm happy. She's still married to the male model, has two children which makes me a grandfather…and I am totally in love with everyone connected, as she is with her husband and children.

"So she doesn't become a glamorous model. There are other things in life that are a great deal more important!"

I had to agree with his comments.

So You Think You Are An Artist!

By Trisdam Alley

I am an artist. At least I think I am. And I have fellow artists who tell me so although I do not paint.

I know I am an artist because I've been getting a lot of money for my current artistic endeavors.

I can remember how it all started.

I had little yen for this field when I was a kid. I used to do a lot of sketches of people and landscapes in a notebook while attending high school, drawing my fellow classmates. My teacher saw my notebook after I had fallen asleep in his class, woke me up and said I must really be interested more in art than what he was teaching in history. He advised I take art classes. I did, and I also joined the committee working on the Senior Class yearbook. I did a lot of sketches for that publication.

After it was published, my parents saw my artwork and then encouraged me to switch majors and go to an art school. I went to the Phoenix School on a scholarship.

Besides reading a lot of art books and articles there, I was taught to think like an artist. That means looking at things more closely than most people do. Finding beauty in everyday things and situations. Making new connections between different things and ideas. Going beyond ordinary ways of thinking and doing things. Looking at things in different ways in order to generate new perspectives. Taking risks and exposing myself to possible failure. Arranging things in new and interesting ways. Persisting where others may give up. Concentrating my effort and attention for long periods of time. Dreaming and fantasizing about things. Doing something simple because I thought it interesting and personally challenging to do.

You know, people often think of artists as painting pictures. At Phoenix, however, I learned that being an artist involves much more than simply 'making pictures.' Artists are curious individuals who are driven by a desire to create and a willingness to take chances. They have a special way of seeing and thinking about the world which is shared with others through the works they create.

I've always been asked *how often do you do it?* How do you *come up such crazy ideas?* The instructors at the school taught and I learned from books connected with my courses that artists often get their best ideas from everyday, ordinary experiences. Eating the morning breakfast can be an opportunity to begin your day of *thinking like an artist*. You eat breakfast and all of a sudden a lion bursts out of your fork. How could that happen? It could have been supercharged by the sweet sugar you put in the cereal you may be eating!

Thinking like an artist sometimes means making the familiar become strange, the ordinary extraordinary. My instructors used to say, go through picture magazines looking for things that might suggest an "outrageous idea.' Don't go for the first idea which is usually boring. Cut out several pictures from a magazine and they try different combinations after you cut the original background away from some of the images you need. Consider changing size relationships, and try putting things together we don't usually see together. When you finish, put a title to this new picture and show it to someone. If they say… "that's outrageous…my instructors said to tell them it's *artrageous*.

Despite the conception of the artist as an isolated, solitary soul, similar to a novelist, I guess, artists recognize their need to exchange ideas and look inside themselves and interact with their times. The opportunity of becoming a member of the art community will also help the artist grow since he will be receiving comments from his fellow artists about his work. It's a very important part of becoming an "artist"…the ability to take criticism because you'll get a lot of it, my teachers warned me.

As my Phoenix teachers taught me from their considerable experience, talent is not worth a thing without work. Given the work, the talent and the opportunity, real artists don't waste it away. They work at it and don't put their art on hold for too long. Armed with talent, knowledge and instinct, the artists enters the world in which it is almost impossible to make a living doing what he or she knows best. When I was learning the techniques of this chosen lifestyle, teachers never spoke about being a success nor what the artist has gleaned from the media with stories that tell about paintings selling for millions of dollars. What the artist finds in the real world is a calculated indifference, curators too busy to look at new artistic work, dealers too committed to their own crop of artists to take on new ones.

It's hard to tell a budding Van Gogh life is hard in the art world and that it is merchandising that has to be sold to make a living. You can't tell an artist that he may have to find a job to support his art-making creativity. There are zillions of artists trying, however. Look at the tremendous amount of art fairs held throughout the country. Over 600 the last I found on the Internet.

When you attend one you'll see hundreds of booths, thousands of pieces of art displayed for sale. I looked into that route, too. It was so frustrating, I gave up.

That's what happened to me. I couldn't afford to be an artist who just painted to make a living. I had a family to support, a child on the way. That's why I became a graphic artist at an advertising agency. It pays good money, and I can still use some of the learned art techniques to satisfy my creativity cravings!

MY JAVA IS GOING SOUTH

by Sandra Posnert

I truly love coffee.

It's the first thing I drink after getting up.

My husband, Jael, and I were sitting in our new condo's kitchen nook discussing this important drink that we both enjoyed.

"I would love to take a trip to the coffee-growing area to see how it's grown. I know that it originated in Ethiopia when a goat herder discovered coffee after noticing that his goats, upon eating berries from a certain tree, became so spirited that they did not want to sleep at night.

"This story was passed on to Arabs and they were the first not only to cultivate coffee, but also to begin its trade since they were always looking for a drink that did not have an alcoholic connection to it because it was forbidden in their religion. They used the thousands of pilgrims visiting the holy city of Mecca each year to spread the word about this fabulous drink.

"By the 15th century, coffee was being grown in many countries around Asia, Central or South America, the islands of the Caribbean or Pacific, all of whom can trace their heritage to the trees in the ancient coffee forests on the Ethiopian plateau. By the 17ᵗʰ century coffee made its way to Europe and was becoming quite popular across the continent. Today, I understand, it's grown in 50 countries, mostly along the equator."

We both took an extra sip from our coffee cups as a toast to this wonderful drink.

"So where do you want to go," Jael asked.

"I think I would like to go where it was first discovered…on the Ethiopian plateaus."

"Good, I'll call our travel agent to book. When should we go?"

I think we better ask our travel agent when's the best time to go…you know, stuff like best weather and when it's not too crowded.

"Yes, you are right. I'll call now.

Jael got on the phone, and I heard him talking to our travel agent. "Yes, that's right, Ethiopia. Sandy wants to see where coffee beans were discovered….Good, look it up and give me a call back as soon as you can."

A couple hours later the agent returned our call to advise what he found. "The best weather time is during the dry season which usually is from May to September. He told us what he could book, where we would go, and how much it cost. No problem.

I really don't want to describe our trip to you, but it was fabulous. We were gone for two weeks and enjoyed practically every day. There were some tough moments when we had to climb a tree to get close to where the coffee berries grew, but we managed.

When we got home we couldn't wait to tell all about the

trip to our children and friends. They were all fascinated with our descriptions and the pictures we took.

There are highlights I think you might like to hear about coffee, so here goes even though it sounds like I'm a promoter of the drink.

Sandra said, "Coffee trees produce their best beans when grown at high altitudes in a tropical climate where there is rich soil. Such conditions are found around the world in locations along the Equatorial zone. The weather, particularly the amount of rainfall and sunshine, combined with the way the coffee berries are processed, contribute the distinctions between coffees from countries, growing regions and plantations worldwide. The combination of these factors is so complex, that even from a single plantation one finds variation in quality and taste.

"A coffee bean is actually a seed. It takes three to four years for a newly planted coffee tree to begin to bear fruit. The cherries are harvested by either being strip picked (the entire crop is harvested at one time) or selectively picked when only the ripe cherries are harvested by hand; this process is so expensive that only finer Arabica beans are usually picked.

Jael continued the story. "Once picked the cherries must be processed as quickly as possible, either by a dry method or a wet one. I won't go into detail about the processes which includes drying, milling, hulling, polishing, grading & sorting. The milled beans now known as 'green coffee' is shipped in either jute or sisal bags.

" The rest of the story about coffee relates to the roasting and grinding of it for brewing. Storage also plays an important role in making coffee one of the best drinks on earth…especially when you are coffee lovers like we are."

There is one problem coming up; we just saw a news flash come across CNN that the future of coffee is in jeopardy because of the drought possibility in the areas where the coffee is now grown…in 50 years!!! It will affect us when we become ancient seniors. We'll keep our fingers crossed that it doesn't happen.

FRAUDS, FRAUDS EVERYWHERE

by Daniel Strork

It's amazing the number of different types of scams and frauds that are being perpetrated on the public.

I've been keeping track of them through a few websites that cover them…Scambusters.com; Craig's List; Fraudslist.com; consumerfraudreporting org/current; fraud.net; fbi.gov.

Here's the FBI's list of frauds from A to Z: Adoption Scams, Advance Fee Schemes, Anti-Aging Product Fraud, ATM Skimming; Bankruptcy Fraud, Corporate Fraud, Credit Card Fraud, Financial Institution Fraud, Foreclosure Fraud, Funeral Fraud, Gameover Malware, Grandparent Scam, Health Care Fraud, Hedge Fund Fraud, House Stealing, Identity Theft, Insider Trading, Insurance Fraud, Internet Fraud, Internet Pharmacy Fraud, Investment Fraud, Jury Duty Scam, Letter of Credit Fraud, Lottery Scams, Mass Marketing Fraud, Mortgage Fraud, Natural Disaster Fraud, Nigerian Letter or "419" Fraud, Online Auction Fraud, Online Auto Auction Fraud, Online Dating Scams, Online Rental

Housing Scheme, Phishing, Ponzi Schemes, Prime Bank Note Fraud, Pump-and-Dump Stock Scheme, Pyramid Schemes, Ransomare, Redemption/Strawman/Bond Fraud, Reverse Mortgage Scams, Scareware, Securities and Commodities Fraud, Senior Citizen Fraud, Smishing, Social Security Card Fraud, Spear Phishing, Sports Memorabilia Fraud, Staged Auto Accident Fraud, Stock Options Backdating, Surrogacy Scam, Swatting, Telemarketing Fraud, Telephone Denial of Service Fraud, Timeshare Schemes, Vishing, Work-at-Home Scams.... plus some I'm sure are missing.

According to the FBI investigators and its partners, they will be adding more links and information as time goes on, so they recommend to check back often.

That's a mess of scams, schemes, frauds, stealing going on. Some I am very familiar with. However, I see the one I got pulled on me isn't on the list. I would call it the "Travel Agency Fake Trip Scheme." Let me tell you about this one from a very personal point of view.

At one time in my career I worked for a Travel Magazine. One day I got a call from an individual looking for someone to help him put out a Travel Club Newsletter. I said I could help him which I did for about a year. We went on a trip to Italy for six days with his Philadelphia travel club. It was a great trip.

He wanted to expand and found a backer; he also offered us the South Florida franchise, but did not ask for any money. A few months later he called and said everything was through since his backer changed his mind!

I was very disappointed. A few weeks later, I saw an ad in the N.Y. Times classified for someone offering areas for travel club investors. I called, met and bought the local area after checking with some of his other area owners.

That, my dear friends, was the last we ever saw of him. No club, no travel, no nothing. In fact we learned that he had sold my local area to three different individuals! A year later he was caught and sentenced to jail for fraud, plus he was supposed to reimburse all the area club owners. Never happened, and we lost a great deal of money at that time.

Analyzing what occurred, I learned that you have to be very careful who you give your money to even though it looks very legitimate and even with all the checking in the world.

You know what happened last week, I got an E-mail from a company that claimed I won a lot of money on a lottery in their country. They were going to send me a check that I could cash and then return them the service fees and money for the country's taxes. You better believe that I closed that e-mail as fast as my little fingers could go over the keyboard.

P.S. Yep, it was a lottery scam. Do you know how many people fall for it. Lots. I hope you'll never be one of those swindled with this fraud scheme. If it's not that one it may be another. You never know.

RING, RING

by Bob Morse

"Mr. Watson, -- come here -- I want to see you" exclaimed Alexander Graham Bell after he knocked over some battery acid. This story is a matter of dispute. However, Thomas Watson, working in the next room, heard Bell's voice through a wire that was partially immersed in a conducting liquid like mercury, which could be made to vary its resistance and produce an undulating current.

In other words, human speech could be transmitted over a wire. This was on March 10, 1876. Watson had received the first telephone call, and quickly went to answer it.

In 1878, Rutherford B. Hayes was the first U.S. president to have a telephone installed in the White House. And to whom did the commander-in-chief place his first call? Bell, of course, who was waiting for the call some 13 miles away. The president's first words were said to have been, "Please speak more slowly."

With that little bit of history, the telephone business has grown tremendously, and today it's still going strong, but with a different approach.

Slowly, the wired telephone is going out of business. No longer is it or will be the device to transmit voice to another individual.

What's happening today is that the wireless telephone is becoming the dominant voice carrier. The *telephone communications industry* as it is now called encompasses a lot of technology-related businesses. Besides local and long-distance phone services, it includes wireless communications, internet services, fiber optics networks, cable TV networks and commercial satellite communications.

Earlier, it was voice calls that brought money to the operators. Now, voice is taking a backseat, while data and voice have become the core focus areas...with speed and better resolution being the rich multi-media applications.

Huge government expenditures, including the U.S. broadband infrastructure program and similar structural subsidies in other countries, have become a boon for telecom service providers and equipment manufacturers.

Smartphones have become the next generation choice and are increasingly taking over a huge share from the basic mobile handsets. These phones are generally characterized by very powerful operating systems capable of supporting a variety of services and applications that need very high-speed network infrastructures.

All this upheaval has affected jobs, investments, and world-wide competition.

The next competitive opportunity started when "Ring, Ring" took over the Morse Code which is now being focused on 3G wireless technologies, emerging 4G technologies, broadband and fiber-to-the-home/premises networking.

Inventions in the industry are still coming at a fast pace. I'm sure that eventually the telecommunications industry, and definitely wired phones, will disappear completely as well.

Who knows what will happen next with the familiar "Ring, Ring" arena? It is impossible to conceive of exactly what future technology might even be like. For example, some predict that preventive medicine will advance to using genetic therapy, and then advance to using genetic therapy. Others say that cloning human organs or operating on your DNA will be a common medical procedure

One thing for sure. Communication technology will most certainly improve by leaps and bounds...even to implanting equipment that will allow people to understand any written language, and even keep abreast of the latest news and weather conditions.

Technology today follows the similar dreams that Mr. Bell and Mr. Watson used then. Finding a solution to problems (in Mr. Bell's case it was helping the deaf).

There's another old saying, "You ain't seen nothing yet." It applies here, too!

WHERE DID MY LITTLE DOG GO?

by Donna Wong

I loved my dog, Yuki.

I don't know what happened to her after she ran away and got lost. We didn't see or find her for about six months.

One day, she did come back, from God knows where.

She had a scar over one ear and unmistakable signs of some kind of stress the vet said.

I have to tell you that our family was one of those who had lived in the Japanese town of Fukushima. You know, the one that turned into a ghost town after the nearby nuclear plant was damaged by the tsunami and eventually caused a lot of problems for us.

It was bad enough that we saw our house float away, but when we couldn't find Yuki, we were really distressed. She had been with us for seven years. You can really become attached to a dog. It gives nothing but love throughout its whole life. We could have used that after we had to leave our home of 40 years. It's known as dog social behavior.

She would use certain movements of her body parts to express her emotions…with the ears, eyebrows, mouth, nose, head, tail and entire body. Even with vocalizations like barks, growls, whines and whimpers and howls, she let us know exactly how she felt.

One of Yuki's body movements, I remember, was with her tail. When her tail was high it showed that she was alert and aware. The tail between her legs meant she was afraid or frightened. If the fur on her tail was bristled, she was saying she was willing to defend herself.

While she didn't bare her teeth much, or curl her lips back, it showed that she had a strong urge to bite. Even her ears would relate to the level of attention she desired. When they were erect and facing forward it meant she was very attentive. Laid back showed a submissive state.

Even mouth expressions can provide information about a dog's mood. When she wanted to be left alone, she yawned. When she was happy and wanted to play, she would pant with lips relaxed, covering the teeth and had what appeared to be a happy expression, occasionally with her mouth open.

Licking also was part of her self-grooming, and also a way of greeting someone who came to visit. Of course, it also meant *I love you*.

As far as her feet and legs, she would stamp her feet, alternating its left and right front legs, while the back legs were still. She would do this when she was excited sometimes, or wanted our attention. It was also common of her to paw or scratch objects she desired.

But to get back to Yuki's return. We were lucky in that

respect because an unknown quantity of dogs were left chained or abandoned amid the disaster we faced in that earthquake and subsequent tsunami of March 11, 2011.

Scientists reported that stray and abandoned animals that recovered near the Fukushima Dai-ichi power station had level of the stress hormone cortisol that were far higher than dogs not exposed which caused them the inability to bond with people who were also experiencing PTSD (post traumatic syndrome).

How long it will take Yuki to rebond with me and the family is an unknown. Yuki has what the vets call *chronic stress.*

All I know is that we humans affected by the disaster are already recovering and gradually returning to a normal life. However, researchers suggest the possibility that stress can induce excessive, deep psychosomatic impacts in dogs.

I love my Yuki, always will, no matter what kind of disease she has. She is just another member of the family forever and I know where she is and *not gone anymore.*

BEAUTY IS ONLY SKIN DEEP!

By Delores Taube

"What's new, Claire. You look years younger."

"Yeah, Delores, it's a new anti-aging cosmetic regime the beauty company I work for introduced a few months ago."

"But, you're not that old yet that you have to worry about wrinkles."

"It doesn't make any difference how old you are, you should start fighting them before they start. My addiction to the epitome of beauty started right after I got married. Youth-looking skin continues to be a huge market all over the world as men and women look for new ways to fight the signs of aging skin. Do you realize that it is a world-wide business of $350 billion?"

Claire asked, "Where did you hear that?"

"Well, Delores, it really all started when I was in my senior year at college and I was taking a history course in ancient civilizations. One of the segments my professor discussed was what the ancients did about beauty. I learned that the ancient Egyptians and the Chinese were the first to document their attempts to halt the relentless march of time, noting the effects of certain types of herbs, mineral treatments, diet and exercise on the condition of the skin, all destined to stop the inevitable first wrinkles and keep young and beautiful looking. Today it has developed into a complex study of molecular biology, botany and even philosophical and psychological research."

Delores interrupted Claire's spiel about when beauty had started, and asked, "What else did you learn that would want me to start a hold-the-wrinkles-back campaign?"

"I'm not trying to sell you anything, Delores," Claire responded, "But if Alchemists spent centuries looking for the 'Elixir of Life'—the mythical ingredient that would grant them access to the 'fountain of youth' and eternal life, there must be something to it. Even today, chemists in the industry are looking back to the Egyptian use of olive oil as part of the beauty treatment program that was used in that era.

"Do you realize what the impact of television had on the beauty industry? With everyone in the U.S. and other advanced countries, it drove beauty advertising sharply upwards. Charles Revson was a master of using the new medium to grow brands. Now it's the shopping channels like HSN and QVC that have become important places to launch new brands."

"I know, I watch them a lot," said Delores.

Claire continued. "The evolution of beauty products really started with soap; that technology was known for thousands of years but was rarely used for personal washing. In the 19th century with water now being pumped directly into homes, the demand for soap was linked to romantic success. It also happened in the perfume part of the beauty business.

"Do you realize that the use of beauty products in China in the 1980s was close to zero; today it's the world's fourth-largest market and the top brands in cosmetics and skin are just like those in the U.S."

"Thanks for the history lesson," Delores said, "But I still need some proof that I should start now before the wrinkles start to set in."

"Very simple," Claire countered. "We have realized that we can't stop the aging process, but we sure can slow it down. That's the process that the cosmetic industry has taken. It makes sense to me."

"Now that I'll buy. What can I use from you?

"Oh, I forgot. Don't let's talk about beauty and cosmetic surgery. That's another part of keeping your skin and body looking younger. I've also have a great surgeon for you............"

STEALING OUR JOBS

by Frank Fraslo

"I lost my job today to a robot," my poker-playing friend Bart stated with a worried look on his face while we took a break during our game.

"Hey, buddy, why not look into a different type of job. You could be a model for robots, ha, ha."

"What do you mean," he replied.

"Just kidding. Today we are all worried about outsourcing our jobs overseas. However, there is a bigger problem that is slowly sneaking up on us. No, not computers which we know has replaced a lot of typewriters, as well as the personnel using them throughout the world. It's the world of robotics: medical robotics and prosthetics; cognitive robotics; intelligent vehicles. In the industrial sections which most benefit from robotics R&D achievements in terms of their competiveness will be: industrial automation, mechatronics, services to citizens for quality of life, and automotive, transportation, personal mobility.

"In surveys I've seen, healthcare and disasters and accidents prevention and managements are considered as the main grand societal challenges and it was suggested that research should mainly focus on improved control schemes, new sensors and actuators, better Human-robot interfaces.

"Some of the robotic dreams of years ago in science fiction are coming true rather quickly. However grand societal challenges in which robotics might play a leading role in the next decade, and in the loss of jobs as it expands, are in healthcare, aging and social distress, independent living, care for the environment and energy, and public services.

"Current research indicates that what R&D shall focus on in the next decade include cognitive robotics, intelligent vehicles, wearable robotics and lots more. Those industrial sectors that will benefit from R&D in robotics are services to citizens for quality of life, home automation, food to name a few."

"Recently I learned from the Internet that a rugged, bipedal humanoid robot, "PETMAN" was created by a Massachusetts company, Boston Dynamics. A video of the robot shows it remaining upright after receiving a stiff shove, performing push-ups, and moving at the pace of a brisk jog. During the demo, the humanoid reached speeds of 4.4 mph."

My friend looked a bit complexed at the story I was telling him. "What has that got to do with me?"

"Well, you were in the service, weren't you?"

"Yes, so what."

"Did you know that it's a short step from these robots to robot soldiers. They can go anywhere when they are perfected. These machines will go anywhere marines go. Combine a better PETMAN with a robot-operated rifle or machine gun and precise target acquisition system for small platforms (which already exist) and you have a robotic soldier.

"In fact. one Japanese company has introduced one for the military market called the *Sarcos exoskeleton*. It is a powered exoskeleton robot that shadows the natural motions of the human body, and can be used to lift 200 pounds as if it were ten.

"Didja know that the 2001 U.S. Congress mandated that one third of all military ground vehicles be unmanned (robotic) by 2015. The industry is currently laying the groundwork to reach this goal.

"In another part of the business, Japan, where robots are culturally accepted, applications for household use are under rapid development. In 2011, a robot nicknamed RIBA II was introduced and was capable of lifting a patient weighing up to 176 pounds off a futon and onto a wheelchair. It was especially interesting to caretakers for the elderly there since they have to perform this task as many as 40 times a day, This robot was different in that it is soft to touch.

"It's easy to downplay the achievements of modern robotics because they mostly operate behind the scenes, in factories and warehouses."

"Okay. You convinced me that robots are the coming thing. I still want to know what that has got to do with me?"

"Why not switch from that crummy, competitive field you were in that hasn't changed in a hundred years. Get into robotics, somehow. There are parts in that industry that will never be changed for humans, one that cannot be replaced by a robot"

"What do you mean?"

"Well, a few days ago I saw a job being advertised for individuals who wanted to get into the robotic field for a great future. This company was looking for salespersons to get involved, learn all about the field, and go out and sell the world on possible performances."

"Hmm," my poker-playing friend said, "You may be right. What was the name of the company looking for real people to help the robots get out into the real world more? I'm sure a robot is not going to replace a real good salesperson, are they? And it's a sure bet one won't be outsourced overseas, either!"

How To Get Pi-Eyed

by John Forth

I called my favorite friend, a math teacher, and told him that a mathematics museum had opened on 12/12/12, which sounded from the date like it was quite neat.

"Ben, did you hear about the new math museum that opened in New York City?"

"Yes," he said, "I've donated some money to the creators to help get it started.

"What can you tell me about it?"

"Well," Ben continued, "It has a mathematical art gallery showcasing changing exhibits that explore the relationship between math and art. There are activities that highlight the role of mathematics in our society and reveal the connections between math and music, math and literature, and math and finance. And, it has a simple history of mathematics and how it started

"The museum, called MoMath, is located at 134 West 26th Street in New York City, which is between Fifth and Madison Avenues."

"Sounds interesting," I replied. "Could you give me a short history about how math started and what's happening with it today? I'm trying to get my son interested in the subject, especially since I know there is a shortage of math teachers, so he wouldn't have trouble finding and keeping a job in that specialty."

"You are right about there being a shortage because it is not an easy subject. In fact most kids in school hate it, and we teachers keep looking for a way to make it 'jazzy' and easy to understand. So far, we have a long way to go.

"However, I can give you a history and what's happening today, but it will take a little time. Call me when you think we will both have the time."

"Thanks. I'll call." Boy was I ever sorry I said I would call!. I did some research on the Internet and found out that it would be a long history lesson, and the prospects of getting my son interested would take some time to convince him to go down that road. However, you have to try when it comes to your children

---

Bill and I were sitting in my den ready to have a talk about mathematics a few weeks later.

"The history of mathematics is interesting if you would want to teach it. While it started long ago, the oldest known possibly mathematical object is the Lebomo bone, discovered in Swaziland and dated to approximately 35,000 B.C. It consisted of 29 notches cut into a baboon's fibula which showed the earliest demonstration of sequences of prime numbers or a six month lunar calendar. There are other findings from Africa and France that suggest early attempts to quantify time.

"Many countries and people were involved in early math, including the Babylonians, Greeks, Egyptians, Chinese, Islamics. From the Middle Ages bursts of mathematic creativity were often followed by centuries of stagnation. The Renaissance in Italy started a new era of mathematical creativity. I won't go into each step in mathematics, but go to Wikipedia on the Internet and check the stories there for more details," Ben continued.

He paused for a few minutes to catch his breath, but you could see he truly loved his subject. "In the 19th century, math became increasingly abstract, while in the 20th century it became a major profession. All of the disciplines in the subject, algebra, calculus, geometry, logic, numbers, statistics, trigonometry, writing numbers, prime numbers, irrational numbers…and education are growing ever larger, especially since computers are more important and powerful."

Ben paused again in his dissertation on mathematics. "Can I have a glass of water, please," he asked. I went to the kitchen to get him one, returned, and he grabbed the glass and quickly consumed its contents.

"That's better," he said. "Now where was I. Oh, yes, continuing the history of mathematics. "My suggestion would be to go to that new museum, MoMath. I think you'll get a better description about not only the history, but what's in the future on the subject.

As a conclusion to our discussion about mathematics, Ben said, "You know, of course, that (pai) is probably one of the most symbols used in mathematics It is a constant that is the ratio of a circle's circumference to its diameter and is equal to 3.14159. It even got a celebration day named after it.

"One could say also it's a way to get a little pi-eyed (intoxicated) on the subject of mathematics!"

WHAT'S HOT / WHAT'S NOT

by Joyce Trainer

"The topic for today, class, is to research and write a paper on the types of deserts in the world. You have a week to check it out, and write an essay about them."

Johnny, a smart eight year old, who was the teacher's favorite pupil, had a great time checking out this subject in the encyclopedias, and on the Internet for the first few days of reading about deserts.

After jotting down a few notes, and preparing an outline to help him write a report, this is what he composed and then handed into the teacher.

DESERTS AROUND THE WORLD
There are many types of deserts around the world.
There are trade wind deserts, midlatitude deserts, rain shadow deserts,. coastal deserts, monsoon deserts, polar deserts, paleodeserts, and extraterrestrial deserts. I've never seen one.
There are 23 main deserts. There are more not on my list because they are ones found in colder climates like the Arctic

Circle and the Antarctic which also aredeserts, albeit cold ones.

The four main things that make a desert are: high pressure regions, dry air currents, rain shadow and cold ocean currents, whatever that means.

A desert is a region which receives very little rainfall which makes little vegetation. The Sahara is the world's largest desert and mainly looks like lots and lots of sand. Usually there are low or no people living in a desert.

I would not like to live in a desert. It probably doesn't have TV, and I can't go roller skating or blading.

Besides, if there are no friends there, how can I enjoy myself.

I asked my mom if she would like to live there. She said no. You know why she said "no." She told me later. She would rather have desserts (ha, ha) in her life than the desert places I described.

Me, too. Horray for desserts...that's what I like also. Hundreds of them, but not all at the same time. You can forget about deserts. They are not an "in" place, but desserts are positively "in".

Harvey Brown, Third grade.

MICKEY'S CALLING

by Joe Mauer

The phone rang. It was seven in the morning. I wondered who would be calling me so early. The sun was just rising so the room wasn't that dark. I could see the phone easily. I picked it up.

"Hello."

"This, Mr. Orlove, is Mr. Lattimon, from Walt Disney World. I hate to bother you so early, but we were concerned whether or not you were going to make it down here by Saturday for your wedding. What with that big storm off your neck of the woods, we hoped everything was okay."

"Was far as I know," Orlove replied slowly since he was still half groggy having been woken so early. "That storm, Randy, hasn't come ashore yet. If anything happens, we'll let you know. As far as we are concerned, it is supposed to hit land about 100 miles from us. Of course, this is only Tuesday, but we are watching it too."

"That's good news. We have been checking the weather station down here and they're all predicting it will be a blockbuster of a storm. How many guests are outside of your area?"

"Well, we expect 87 people who said they would be coming to the wedding. Most are from here, and there are about 15 coming from other parts of the country. I don't believe they will be affected by this storm. Those around this area might be if it is as bad as they say it is, and air flights get to be cancelled. Right now, we'll play it by ear and see what happens."

"All right," Lattimon said, "But if you are going to have any trouble let us know as soon as possible." He hung up.

We had made plans to hold our wedding at the Waldorf Astoria Orlando hotel and resort near Walt Disney World, and my fiancée had just picked up her wedding dress the night before. So, we were ready. I quickly turned on the TV to catch the weather.

"This is Bill Ardmore of station WFNZ weather reporting on what's happening to this huge hurricane sweeping close to our area. Called Randy, it is reported that it has winds of 125 miles per hour, with tornadoes and gusts up to 175. That's pretty strong. The coastal area has been evacuated, and those 25 to 50 miles from where the center is going to strike have been warned to button up, or get out, too. Stay tuned, we will keep you posted every half hour."

That didn't sound so good. I had to get in touch with my fiancee, Lila, to talk over the situation. I dialed her.

"Hey, it's me. I hear your TV in the background, so you are probably up to date with that hurricane's location as I am. What do you think we should do…Yes, I agree. I think we should get out of here asap. But what about our guests. I wonder if they plan to fly because they're reporting that most air flights have been cancelled. If this is the case, I have an idea of how to get everyone out of here and to Florida before it's too late…Come on over, and we'll discuss it."

About an hour later Lila and I met. We made plans. Here's what we decided to do. We would have to call everyone from this area to meet us at one place and travel together…not by plane, not by train since they too had cancelled all departures from this area. No, we decided to rent two buses to carry all the 56 who were leaving from here before the storm arrived. But, we would have to do it pretty quickly since we figured it would take at least two days to drive down.

We divided our guest list up and made all our calls in an hour. Everyone we called knew their flights were cancelled and were thinking how to get to Florida. Our call solved their problem

At the end of the day, all our guests were on the two rented buses at the bus terminal and we were ready to go. The only thing was that Lila and I had trouble getting to the bus terminal. We hit the advance rain from the storm, and our car stalled about a mile away. We knew we would have to walk/run, which we started to do. I had her dress over my head, and she carried a small suitcase. We practically ran all the way to the terminal; we got there on time.

The buses left Wednesday evening about 7 pm and ended up at the Disney hotel on late Thursday. Everyone was comfortable, and had one day of rest before the wedding.

As the sun set behind the trees at the wedding site,

Lila and I held hands and said "I do" in front of all the wedding guests outside the hotel...no rain, winds or tornados spoiled our wedding.

We kissed, fireworks went off in the clear Central Florida sky. All was right with the world.

The lesson we learned from this experience was "if there is a will, there is a way!"

MAKE SURE YOUR CAR FITS

By Jerry Canberg

I've been driving ever since I was 17. I'm just about to become a "Senior". That means I'll be 67 (the new age limit now for a definition of a SENIOR according to the Social Security Administration) very shortly, which means I've been driving almost 50 years!

Does that say I know everything I should know about driving as a senior? According to a program put out by the AARP called "Car-Fit", I really don't.

One thing I found out from a survey, older drivers are more likely to wear their seatbelts, are less likely to speed or drink and drive. However, at least one in ten seniors are seated too close to the steering wheel, at least four do not have line of sight at least three inches over the steering wheel, and almost three have at least one critical safety issue that needs addressing.

Let me explain some of the things this program does that shows you there are many things we all should know and make adjustments to before becoming a "Senior!" Let's look at them and what we have to check and precautions to take:

1. Have a clear line of sight over the steering wheel. At least three inches above the top of the wheel.
2. Make sure there is plenty of room between your breastbone (or chest) and the air bag in the steering wheel...10 inches minimum to let the bag deploy.
3. A driver's seat you fit in comfortably and safely. You should be able to adjust the seat for good visibility and easy access to controls.
4. Properly adjusted head restraint. Prevents neck injury. Restraint's center should be about three inches or less from the center of the back of your head, not against your neck.
5. Easy access to gas and brake pedals. Should be able to reach them without having to stretch too far, and you should be able to completely depress the brake pedal and be able to move your foot easily from the gas to the brake.
6. A seat belt that holds you in the proper position and remains comfortable as you drive. Lap belt should be placed low across your hips, and the shoulder belt should cross mid-shoulder and across your chest. A seat belt should never go behind your back or under your arm. You should be able to reach the shoulder belt and buckle and unbuckle the seat belt without difficulty
7. You should be able to get into and out of your vehicle easily

8. Be able to turn you head to look over your shoulder when changing lanes and backing up
9. Sit comfortably without knee, back, hip, neck or shoulder stiffness or pain.

One of the most important things you must do is adjust your mirrors to greatly reduce blind spots. Adjust the rear view mirror so it shows as much of the rear window as possible. While in the driver's seat, place your head near the left window and adjust the left-side view mirror so you can see the side of your vehicle. Then position your head near the middle of the car, above the center console, and adjust the right side-view mirror so you can just see the side of your vehicle.

To achieve all these new suggestions, you may need adaptive devices such as seat belt extenders, visor extenders, steering wheel covers, larger rear-view mirrors, pedal extenders and others devices.

The Car-Fit program really helped me out. I did all these things it said to do…but, unfortunately in vain.

I went to renew my driver's license right after I finished all this protective work. Wouldn't you know, I failed because my eyesight, even with glasses, had gone so bad I was prohibited from driving any more.

That's the way life is. You never know what's going to happen next!

JIM & JAN LUCKY INC.

By Bernard Block

Our first hint that we were involved with a scam is when we received a call from Mexico.

We saw the area code that was not familiar to us as the number 744 popped up before the other seven numbers.

Our experience with these out-of-the-country calls was that they were nothing more than trouble.

Later, we checked our phone directory and found that the area code indicated the call was from Acapulco, Mexico.

In our business, publishing newsletters, we knew we did not have any clients in this part of the world, nor any relatives either.

Under those circumstances, of course, we did not pick up and answer the ring. We've been warned by too many sources that if you don't know them, you don't answer them.

A few days later, a strange e-mail came from the Mexican Dept. of Treasury. We didn't open that one either. While it sounded very official with the subject matter listing dollars due, we had no one we knew in Mexico, nor did we have any transactions there that involved money. Definitely knew it was a scam working.

Those strange e-mails kept coming practically every day for a week.

About a month later, we received a call from our lawyer who had incorporated us 40 years ago. He asked us why we were not answering our Mexican calls.

"How, Bob, did you know we were getting e--mails from Mexico?"

"I got a call from a fellow accountant who lives in Mexico to advise that the government was trying to reach you."

"Did he tell you what they wanted?"

"No, but they said it was important that they talk to you. It was something about shale gas."

What the hell do I or Jan have to do with shale gas. It still sounded like a scam.

Out of curiosity, I looked in an encyclopedia about shale gas in Mexico. Here's what I found out.

Mexico's massive shale gas deposits could be profitably extracted if North American natural gas prices continue rising toward $4 per million cubic feet, said an official with state oil monopoly Pemex

The country boasts the world's fourth-largest reserves of shale gas in deposits that may contain rich pockets of both natural gas and oil.

A Pemex executive said they saw the potential of shale oil which is trapped in rocks and requires expensive technology called hydraulic fracturing, or fracking, to unleash. He said this year they will be drilling two wells to prove the existence of more profitable shale oil. The company has already drilled four shale gas wells in the country's Burro-Picachos field, an extension of the Eagle Ford shale formation near the U.S.-Mexico border, plus two nearby.

Interesting, but what has that go to do with us?

It was time to go on vacation, so Jan and I had to make a decision of where we wanted to go.

"How about Acapulco?" I said. "We could combine a vacation with a visit to their Treasury Department located there and see what they have been calling us about."

"Not a bad idea, as long as we enjoy our vacation first before we get involved with the Mexican government."

We started to plan our Mexican vacation. We hadn't been there for 40 years, so it would be a 'what's new' vacation in this vibrant neighboring country.

There was plenty to see in Acapulco. There were the usual cliff divers; Fort of San Diego; Zocalo and its old parts; bungee jumping; parasailing, balloon rides, a giant swing (Skycoaster); themed water parks, to name a few.

We called the Treasury Department to see the man who worked with foreigners, Senior Lopez.

As we entered his office, he greeted us with a big smile and said, "So glad to meet you Mr. & Mrs. Lucky. We have been trying to reach you for the past few months, but never could. We did send you e-mails, but I guess you never opened them because of scams and frauds that prevail so regularly on those Internet sites.

"Believe me, what I am about to tell you is not a fraud or scam. It's reality at its best.

"Do you remember what you did 40 years ago when you incorporated your business here in Mexico to take advantage of our very low taxes, and the extra bonus we tempted you with?"

"No, not really," Jim and Jan replied simultaneously. "What did we do?"

"When you incorporated your company here through your accountant's suggestion, you received a bonus…a tract of land's mineral rights. Remember now?"

"Holy smokes,", Jan said, "I really forgot about that bonus; it's been so long ago. What's happened?"

"You've lived up to your name of Lucky," Lopez said. "That tract of land you received is one of the places that our shale gas wells are being drilled. First reports is that it could be very productive. If it is, you are going to become millionaires."

Both Jan and Jim jumped up and high fived to celebrate. "What do you know, we're going to be rich!"

"Do you want to see your land", Lopez asked after the Lucky's calmed down.

"Why not," they both replied in unison.

"Good, I'll arrange transportation to the spot. It's near the Eagle-Ford area which is close to the U.S. border. What day would you like to go? It should take a couple of hours by private limo we'll supply to get you there."

"I guess a week from now would be okay. We can extend our vacation now that we are going to be millionaires."

"I'll arrange everything," Lopez stated. "I'll call you and let you know when our driver will pick you up, and make sure there is a guide at the site to take you to the well on your site."

Ramuel, our Mexican shale-well guide, met our limo at the main road leading to our land where we owned the mineral rights. We switched to his SUV for a short ride on a side road.

"Before I show you the exact spot that the well will be sunk, let me explain how the whole shale-gas process works.

"The process of bringing a well to completion is generally short-lived, taking a few months for a single well to be completed and can be in production for 20 to 40 years. The process for a single horizontal well typically takes four to eight weeks to prepare the site for drilling, four or five weeks of rig work, including casing and cementing and moving all associated auxiliary equipment off the well site before fracking operations commence, and two to five days for the entire multi-stage fracturing operation.

"Hydraulic fracturing has played an important role in the development of oil and natural gas resources for nearly 60 years. In the U.S., an estimated 35,000 wells are hydraulically fractured annually. Each well is a little different and each one offers lessons learned. Fracturing makes it possible for shale oil extraction to produce oil and natural gas in places where conventional technologies are ineffective. It uses water pressure, under tight controls, to create fractures in rock that allow oil and natural gas it contains to escape and flow out of a well."

"That sounds interesting," Jim said, "But I guess you can't see it from up here, can you.?"

"Of course not; however, you can see results when the oil or gas reaches the top. The remainder of the site is restored to its original condition and the environmental benefits, such as reducing air and greenhouse gas emissions, last for decades. Local impacts, such as noise, dust and land disturbance, are largely confined to the initial phase of development."

We walked around the site, and secretly blessed the land for holding such wonderful money-making fuels below, land that we had mineral rights that we obtained 40 years ago. We spent about an hour very quietly enjoying each minute.

"Time to go," said Ramuel. We walked back to the SUV, and then climbed back into our limo to end what we considered a perfect day.

When we got home, we called all our friends and family and told them what happened. However, we decided to keep going with our business until we started to see royalty checks coming in for our mineral rights. In fact we checked with our lawyer to learn all about these rights.

He explained it this way since most people do not know how mineral rights work.

"How you achieve a piece of property has nothing to do with mineral rights unless you give a good reason why they should. From what you tell me, you were given these rights by the Treasury Department of Mexico as a bonus for registering your business corporation in their country. You probably didn't understand what the benefit of this bonus was, but it didn't cost you anything so you completely forgot about it.

"No matter how you got these rights wherever they were, if you owned them, and you should have some papers covering this situation, you are entitled to collect a royalty on all the gas found on the property in most cases.

I would suggest you call the Mexican official you saw and ask him if it is a royalty, can you transfer it to your inheritors. One thing you must make sure. Do you retain these rights by keeping your business account in force and active. What happens if you don't?

"I would surmise that your rights will cease when you no longer are renewing your corporate account there. Check out your papers."

———

We listened to our lawyer describe the mineral rights situation, and tried to remember where we put any papers that described the bonus for registering our corporation in Mexico.

You must remember, it's 40 years ago, and both Jane and I can't recollect ever seeing those papers. All we remember about the corporation is that we have a paper with a Mexican identification-registration, and a corporate seal to imprint our Corporate name on any documents… which, by the way, we can never remember using it.

Now the hardest part is to find all the original papers connected with our registration. The first thing is that we have to remember where they are since we have not seen them, or looked for them, since the very beginning. It would take time.

And time it took. Since we had moved three times in the past 40 years, we had to go through all our paperwork connected to our corporation, *Jim & Jan Lucky Inc.* I can remember how hard it was to find all our reports when we were audited once by the IRS for income taxes, and the same year by the state for our sales tax reports about twelve years ago. But to go back 40 years. Wow.

Two months later, in the last box we looked in we found what we needed. Funny part, it was at the very bottom of the box right below the corporate seal.

The most important thing that bothered me was why we incorporated in a foreign country. It was not because we were trying to hide a lot of money like if you opened a bank account in the Cayman Islands, for instance.

Well, anyway, we found it, read the documents, and saw that we did receive a bonus of mineral rights in the part of Mexico that were supposed to have a lot of oil. We called our lawyer and read him the whole document.

"Congratulations," he said. "You might turn into millionaires. When you get your first check, call me."

It arrived, the first check, six months later. The amount was $100,560 to cover royalties for the past month.

We both jumped with joy right after I opened the envelope with the check, and an analysis of how they calculated the amount. We, of course, did not understand it all, but what the heck, money found is not to be questioned.

Right away we booked a cruise, our favorite vacation expenditure, for a few months later. To us, if the checks kept coming like that we certainly would be millionaires. I guess the last name Lucky aptly applied to our new situation.

Just after we came back from our cruise, one of the calls listed on our answering machine showed the number of the Mexican Treasury in Acapulco.

"I wonder what they wanted. Probably we forgot to pay some taxes on that income we got from the gas royalties, although I never heard anyone mention that there was one in Mexico. I know we would have to declare this income on our U.S. forms, but I wouldn't complain too much," I said to Jan.

"Never mind questioning me, "call that Mr. What's-His-Name at the Treasury Dept. there, and do it right away."

"His name was Lopez, I think. I'll call right now."

I dialed the number and waited. Finally, someone answered. I asked for Mr. Lopez. They asked me why I was calling. I told them that they called me a few days ago but I was on vacation and just got back.

The person on the phone told me to hold on. I waited, and waited, and waited. Finally after about ten minutes a familiar voice got on the phone.

"Mr. Lopez, how can I help you?"

"Hi, Mr. Lopez. Remember me. Jim Lucky. Remember, I'm the mineral rights guy in the United States you talked to months ago and told me all about my good luck due to the shale-gas strike on the property I was given by your government because I opened a corporate account in your country."

"Well, Mr. Lucky, I have some news for you and it isn't too good," Mr. Lopez stated. "That wonderful mine we found on your property has not been continuing to produce the amount of gas that it was supposed to. In fact, the engineers at the site are saying the gas is drying up, a common occurrence at shale-producing wells. We'll get the final report in about a month. It may be necessary to close the well if that is the case. Sorry about that. I'll let you know if the situation changes."

I didn't know whether to laugh or cry. Mr. Lucky wasn't so lucky anymore.

THE
END
Or is it?

Look for the next edition…

THE SHORT, SHORT-STORY

...Omnibus-2

Coming July 2013

PUBLISHER'S NOTE: A printed version of Omnibus-1 is available. Contact the publisher at karadenll@juno.com. **Cost is $9.95.**